THE BLACK LOOK

by MICHAEL BUTTERWORTH

The Black Look
Flowers for a Dead Witch
The Uneasy Sun
The Soundless Scream

The Black Look

MICHAEL BUTTERWORTH

Published for the Crime Club
BY
Doubleday & Company, Inc.
Garden City, New York
1972

All of the characters in this book
are fictitious, and any resemblance
to actual persons, living or dead,
is purely coincidental.

Library of Congress Catalog Card Number 76–180064
Copyright © 1971, 1972 by Michael Butterworth
All Rights Reserved
Printed in the United States of America
First Edition

For Victoria Vernon

◀ ONE ▶

IT WAS 12:45 P.M., and BEA Flight 202 from London had landed at Orly airport.

The young Customs officer perched on the baggage counter checked his reflection against a glassy-surfaced column nearby, then switched his gaze to the head of the queue that was beginning to form at the immigration desk. The new arrivals were held up for a few moments by the lunch-time change-over at the desk. The off-duty man came out and walked over toward him.

He was grinning; they shared interests.

"Watch it, Georges!"

"What's that?"

The immigration officer nodded back to the queue, and winked.

"About the fourth one back. Black coat. I'd have stayed to chat her up a bit, but the wife's waiting outside for me in the car."

"Nice?"

The other rolled his eyes, and sketched an hour glass with his hands.

"Superb—what I could see of it."

"Well, now. I'll detain her for a while and give myself an eyeful."

"Don't pervert the authority of the department—but have fun. See you."

"See you, Jules."

The young Customs officer got to his feet, flicking a speck of dust from his braided trousers and tapping his kepi a centimeter to one side, as the first of the new arrivals straggled over from the rotating baggage conveyor.

"Anything to declare, monsieur? Anything to declare, madame?" He marked three sets of luggage, eyes swiveling over their owners' shoulders when he made the inquiry. He picked her out quite quickly.

She was in a patterned dress, with a black coat draped over her shoulders like a cape, and she moved like liquid silk. Big, dark eyes in a pale, oval face framed in long black hair that was partly gathered in a knot at the crown of her head. She paused irresolutely, holding a black hatbox. The huge eyes were searching.

"Here, mam'selle." He tapped the counter in front of him.

There were two others with her: another girl with short blonde hair and horn-rimmed glasses—nice figure also, but the prominent nose and teeth put her right out of her companion's class—a *jolie laide*. And there was a thick-set type in a pink cord battle-dress, with an Indian silk scarf fluttering at his neck. He was burdened down with photographic gear, and gesturing to a porter who had a heavy pile of luggage on his barrow.

"Are you together, mam'selle?" He let his eyes pour down her slender figure, and bet himself a month's pay that she wore no brassiere under the thin dress.

"Yes, we are—the three of us." Her French had only that fashionable trace of the English accent that goes down so well on the Left Bank.

"Have you anything to declare?"

"Nothing at all!" It was the photographer type who replied; but the Customs officer held the girl's gaze.

"What is the purpose of your visit to France, mam'selle?"

The blonde gave a snort of irritation, and muttered something in English about the Common Market. He ignored that, too, and persisted in trying to win a smile from no-bra.

"We're on a photographic assignment—for a magazine," she said evenly. No smile there.

He traced his finger along the edge of the hatbox, and flipped up a leather luggage label attached to the handle. There was a card inside:

Candida Jeans
3a Magdala Mews
Chelsea, S.W.3

He met her gaze again, and gave her the best of his very white teeth, crinkling the corners of his eyes till the sex appeal should have run out like whey.

"Would you open the box, please?"

It was probably the irritable exclamations exchanged between her two companions that softened her. She made a *moue* that ended up as a smile of apology, and opened the lid.

"There's only my make-up and a few odd things," she said. Then, glancing down into the open hatbox, her expression changed.

Lying on top was something bundled in a scarf of red

lace—something that yielded suavely between the Customs officer's fingers as he lifted it out and laid it on the counter.

"And what's this?" he asked, unwrapping it.

"I don't . . . oh, my God!" Her voice died like a spent match.

To him, the first flashing resemblance was to a pig's trotter, lying on a butcher's dish in the covered market near his home. Then it was like a white glove stuffed with lard and bound up with dirty red wool at the wrist.

He gave it another tentative touch—and cold, dead flesh moved across ridges of bone.

It was a severed hand. A real one—because even the plastic ones you can buy in the joke shops don't have such exquisitely modeled fingernails, nor faint pelts of dark hair at the first phalanxes and along the heel of the palm, nor do they express droplets of watery blood from about the white disk of bone at the sliced-off end.

By now, both girls were screaming—and he was staring into the photographer's ashen face that must surely be mirroring his own sudden horror.

That Monday, as always if the weather was decent, Superintendent François René Haquin, of the judicial police, had walked from his office for a solitary lunch at a brasserie off the Place du Chatelet: *sole bonne femme*, a glass of Alsatian beer and a glance through the midday edition. Haquin was no mixer.

By a quarter to two, he was on his way back to the Pont au Change and the gray river that was barred with shifting blue under the patchy April sky, to where his assistant would be waiting for him with a car.

Haquin, a Breton from St. Malo, had served in the Free French navy in the war, and the lower part of his right leg had had to be taken off by a cheerful British surgeon-lieutenant at Haslar Hospital, Gosport, after the torpedoing of his ship and six hours' immersion in the icy Channel. The war had left him with a marginal tendency to Anglophilia, a good command of English, and half an aluminum leg that always let him down on the last stretch back to the Quai des Orfèvres—hence Inspector Martin and the car at the corner of the bridge.

There was no sign of the black Citroën. Haquin spent five minutes placidly thumbing through a book on European birds at one of the riverside bookstalls, before he heard Martin's whistle. The young inspector's head stuck out of the car's nearside window, over-long flaxen hair flopping.

Haquin got into the car, lifting his aluminum leg after him, and they swept out into the traffic.

"Anything going?"

"The strangest thing, Chief," said Martin. "I nearly rang you at the brasserie, but decided it could wait."

"Oh, yes?"

"It started with a call from the Orly police. Customs found a hand in an English girl's hatbox."

"Did you say *hand*—a human hand?"

"Real. Severed"—the young inspector broke off to shout his cheerful speculations on the paternity of a cyclist who wavered close to the Citroën's wing—"and quite fresh, too. Nasty. As soon as it arrived, I sent it straight down to Pathology, with a request for a quick interim report."

"Male or female, the hand?"

"Male, Chief. A right hand."

"And the girl?"

"She's a fashion model. Arrived in on the midday flight from London, with another girl and a male photographer. The model—name of Candida Jeans—is being treated for shock, but the doc says she'll be fit for you to see her in an hour or so. The other two are in the waiting room."

"It's a damned queer thing to carry around in one's luggage," said Haquin. "Have any of the three of them offered any explanation yet?"

"That's the strangest part," said Martin. "The Jeans girl went half out of her mind with the shock and surprise of seeing it there, and her companions are as dumbfounded and horrified as she—and I'd swear their reactions are genuine. No guilt, or anything like it."

Haquin made no reply. He was still silent when they slid into a parking space outside headquarters, and got out. The first splattering of a rain shower made them quicken pace toward the arched doorway, where two uniformed officers on duty were unrolling their capes; they fumblingly saluted the inspector. Rain was already sluicing down behind their heels as Haquin and Martin went up the steps and into the echoing hall that smelled of fresh paint and was spanned by decorators' scaffolding. The Quai des Orfèvres was having a face-lift: workmen in brown paper caps were spraying an institutional, dun-colored paint on the ceiling, and several of them were so unawed by the sacred precincts of the directorate of judicial police as to be whistling.

Haquin glowered up at the figures on the scaffolding, hunched his shoulders, and picked his way across the paint-spotted tarpaulin that carpeted the hall.

"How much longer's this going on?" he growled.

"They'll be finished by June—if there isn't another strike," said Martin placatingly.

Haquin's office was being painted out, and they had given him a second-floor cubbyhole, in which was crammed his desk and Martin's, two filing cabinets, and a pile of dusty dossiers stacked chest high under the single tiny window.

With so little room, the presence of Martin's tennis racquet in a corner (Monday was his tennis night) seemed an intolerable intrusion. And the walking space was further circumscribed by four suitcases and a hatbox piled up between the two desks.

"This is their luggage," said Martin. "Customs have been right through it with a fine comb. No more bits of bodies. No drugs. Nothing."

The keys were in the locks. Haquin opened the black hatbox and looked inside at an untidy array of cosmetics, a black hairpiece in a plastic bag, and a large crêpe-de-chine handkerchief.

"The hand was in there," said Martin. "Lying on top, wrapped in a lace scarf."

The superintendent nodded. Laying aside the hatbox, he snapped open the uppermost case.

"Well, I'm damned!" said Martin.

Nothing but blackness. Haquin lifted out a black woolen jacket. A matching skirt lay underneath it. There were three black shirtwaists and a black dress. At the bottom, another woolen suit and some accessories—tights, scarves, bracelets, necklaces, rings—all in the same ultimate tone.

"Have these people come to Paris to take photographs," said Haquin, "or are they here to attend a blessed funeral?"

The waiting room was on the third floor and faced the Left Bank, with a view across the Luxembourg Gardens to Montparnasse. Save for the English couple, the room was empty; they were standing by one of the windows when the two detectives entered.

Haquin was carrying a slim folder. He briskly introduced himself in English, offered his hand to the man and bowed to the girl.

"My office is in a chaos. Shall we sit at this table?"

They sat down: Haquin facing the couple across a varnished whitewood trestle table that stood in the middle of the room; Martin at the window end, his notebook open, ballpoint poised.

Haquin made a play of opening the folder and sorting a sheaf of typescript that lay inside, and all the time he was assessing the man and the girl.

She looked the capable type, and was probably a very cool customer under normal circumstances—or even under normal stress conditions—but now her eyes were strained and her fingers trembled as she took out a cigarette. Gauloises, he observed, and from an unfamiliar, cellophane-wrapped export packet. Very Chelsea-trendy.

The young fellow's dark hair was in one of the uniform styles favored by the European and American communications industries: half covering the ears and long at the neck, but it was clean and neat. Good fingernails. His shoes were good, too. Presumably successful in his profession. And not a homosexual, either—not if Haquin was any judge. He had the build of a Rugby player.

Haquin cleared his throat, and began without any preamble.

"Now, mademoiselle. You are Sonia Hammersley; unmarried; occupation fashion editor; resident in London? And you, monsieur, are Hilary John Lubbock; unmarried; occupation photographer; residence London?"

"Yes."

"Yes." The man looked at his companion for a split-second before replying, and the significance was not lost on Haquin: Sonia Hammersley was the dominant character of the two—either that or Lubbock had been so excessively well brought up that he always let the lady speak first.

"And your colleague—who is not with us—is Candida Jeans; unmarried; occupation fashion model; resident in London?"

The blonde nodded.

Haquin sat back, and deliberately addressed Lubbock: "Now, what can you tell me about this business?"

He got the reaction he was expecting: the girl replied without any hesitation.

"The whole thing's some sort of ghastly hoax!" she snapped. "Someone must have slipped that . . . object . . . into Candida's box while we were in the bar of the departure lounge at London airport."

"A medical student, perhaps?" said Haquin quietly.

Sonia Hammersley's green eyes flared with relief, and she flashed him a communicative smile that was skillfully controlled to show not too much of her handsome—but slightly prominent—teeth.

"That's *exactly* what I was going to say. They'd have the access, wouldn't they? Let's face it, they cut up bodies as part of their studies. And there was this simply hideous crew of roughneck student types milling round the bar when we were there. Half drunk, and singing bawdy songs."

"These were male students?" asked Haquin.

"Yes," she said. "And of the worst possible roughest type. Any one of them could have slipped the thing into Candida's box while we weren't looking."

"We actually left our hand luggage on a table while the three of us were at the bar," said Lubbock.

"It sounds quite possible," said Haquin, "but let's leave it for now. Tell me more about yourselves as a group. You're in Paris for a photographic assignment, it says here. Tell me about that, please."

Again, Lubbock glanced questioningly at Sonia Hammersley, and it was she who replied. Now she was all professional authority, with the last of her nervousness gone. The fingers that lit another Gauloise were quite steady. It occurred to Haquin that she was a woman who would go far in her career—and heaven help anyone who had the misfortune to be standing in the way of her advancement.

"I am the fashion editor of *Focal*," she said, briskly tapping her cigarette over the ashtray. "*Focal*, the magazine for the woman of taste, published by the Grave Vale Press, London. You've probably heard of it—it has a considerable circulation on the Continent.

"This assignment we're on is for a special autumn issue we dreamed up at a recent editorial meeting: an issue with a special gimmick."

"Autumn?" Haquin's brow crinkled. "This is April. You work all that far ahead, then?"

"Yes." This was with a flat stare of contempt. No explanations for a mere man with no idea of fashion's way of life.

"I'm sorry," said Haquin. "You were saying something about a—gimmick?"

"The Black Look," said Sonia Hammersley.

"Ah, black . . ." Haquin nodded, and caught Martin's sudden glance.

"The special issue will project black as an autumn fashion color," said Sonia Hammersley. "The London *couturiers* have gone rather overboard on black, and it provides us with a peg on which to hang a gimmick. We decided to bring Candida over here and shoot her on location in some of your eerie Parisian cemeteries, in the black ensembles we've brought. You know . . . Père Lachaise, and all that."

"I have never been to Père Lachaise," said Haquin dryly,

"but I believe Inspector Martin has some relations buried there."

Sonia Hammersley looked affronted. "The end product—the issue on the bookstalls—will be in perfect good taste," she said. "There is no question of mocking the dead or anything like that. It's the ambience we're after—the fantastic tomb architecture and the haunting loneliness. And that's why we chose Candida to be model. She has the quiet, haunted look that fits in with the gimmick."

Haquin shrugged, and toyed with the edges of the folder. "I am sure you know your business best, Miss Hammersley. To revert to your colleague Miss Jeans: this affair must have been a considerable shock to her. Would it not, perhaps, be suitable if I arranged for her parents to be informed? Or her fiancé, perhaps?"

"She doesn't have a fiancé, and I'm pretty sure that her parents are dead. Isn't that right, Hilary?"

The photographer nodded. Haquin noticed that a flush of embarrassment had further darkened his ruddy cheeks—and he wondered why.

◀ TWO ▶

SHE LAY on a bunk in a shadowed, antiseptic-smelling room with a long window that looked out across the rain-swept courtyard to the archway through which they had brought her in the back of the police car.

The effect of the tablets they had given her were beginning to wear off. Reality—which had stood apart, so that the familiar world had fused into a shadowgraph—was coming back, and she found that she was able to control it. A small effort of concentration upon the tactile quality of the blanket on which she was lying also sharpened her awareness of the rain splattering on the window panes; when she let her mind drift, the senses of touch and hearing ebbed back into unreality again.

The double-double beat of footsteps ripped through all that. When the door opened noisily, she sat bolt upright. It was the doctor, and there was someone else with him: a stocky man in a dark blue suit.

"Awake, Mam'selle Jeans?" The doctor addressed her in French. He crossed over to the bunk, long face wrinkled in a smile, myopic eyes compassionate behind thick lenses. His fingers closed round her wrist, touching her pulse.

The other man stayed by the door.

"I think you will be all right now. This is my good friend Superintendent Haquin, who would like to have a little talk with you. I will leave you two alone together."

He nodded and went out, closing the door quietly behind him.

Candida Jeans swung her legs down from the bunk, and the linoleum felt cold to the touch of her stockinged feet. She shivered, eyeing the man in the dark blue suit as he limped toward her, dragging a chair with him and setting it in place beside the bunk.

"Well now, mam'selle," he murmured quietly, "you have had a most unpleasant experience, and I don't want to impose on you too much. Just a few points . . . Do you feel in a fit state to talk about it?"

She closed her eyes, and nodded.

"Good. It could wait till tomorrow, but I'd prefer to settle one or two things right away, to assist my inquiries."

Her eyes flared open. "You're going to keep me here?"

He smiled. "No indeed, mam'selle. I have no reason to. It is not a crime, as such, to enter France with a portion of human anatomy, but merely an act that calls for some degree of explanation." He smiled wryly. "No, you can go just as soon as you please—one of your companions is waiting to escort you to your hotel."

She drew a shuddering breath, and looked down at her tensed fingers. Outside, the rain was still coming down, and she heard someone run across the cobbled yard.

"I—I don't know how it got there," she whispered.

"That, also, I am taking into account," he said. "As to how it came to be there, that is something I hope we—our colleagues in London and ourselves—will have settled by the time you leave Paris toward the end of the week. On Thursday, is it not?"

"Yes—Thursday."

He settled back in the chair, hitching his game right leg over the left with both hands, and giving her an expression compounded of guilelessness and impenetrability, so that her frightened mind registered the fact: he's deliberately displaying his hurts, like a lame beggar in an Eastern market, so as to win my trust and sympathy.

He said: "Have you any reason to suppose that anyone would have—er—planted that hand in your hatbox out of malice?"

"No."

"Are you personally acquainted with any medical student, surgeon or physician . . ."—he paused for a moment— ". . . or undertaker? And before you reply, mam'selle, let me put this thought to you—it is simply a theory of mine— this photographic assignment for which you have come to Paris: the Black Look. It is a macabre idea, is it not, to take fashion photos in cemeteries? Supposing, mam'selle, that one of your friends of a certain profession—medical student, surgeon or what have you—and possessing a macabre sense of humor, had put the hand into your box, as a misplaced joke, relating to your assignment?"

She shook her head vehemently. She knew no one who could possibly have done such a thing, and she told him so.

Did she, perhaps, attend a party last night—a farewell party?

"No." But her glance wavered.

"But you went out?"

"No."

"Saturday, perhaps. You went out on Saturday?"

"Yes."

"With a friend?"

"Yes."

"Male, this friend?"

She nodded.

"Could one ask his name?"

Candida Jeans looked down at her hands again, and replied in a small voice: "He's the art director of *Focal* magazine."

"His name, mam'selle," with an edge of persistence.

"Jeremy Stanton."

"At what hour did you return to your flat in—let me see —Magdala Mews?"

"Quite early. About six. We—only went to the zoo for a couple of hours."

"By then, of course, you hadn't packed your luggage for the trip to Paris?"

"No. I did that on Sunday afternoon."

"Including the hatbox?"

"Yes."

"Did anyone call to see you on Sunday? Mr. Stanton, perhaps?"

She shook her head.

Haquin got awkwardly to his feet and touched her briefly on the shoulder. "There, you see, that is all I am going to ask you today. Not too bad, was it? Now your colleague, Mr. Lubbock, is waiting to take you to your hotel. Rest awhile, mam'selle, and I will send him down with my assistant and arrange for a car to take you there."

He crossed over to the door; paused there, looking reflectively back at her.

"You speak excellent French, mam'selle. You were, perhaps, educated here?"

"No," she said. "I had the groundings from a very good teacher who was French. She . . . took a special interest in me."

"With good cause, I fancy. You must have applied yourself very diligently to your lessons to have achieved such competence."

Then he was gone, his limping tread fading off down the passage beyond the door.

Suddenly weary, she let her head fall back against the pillow—and some memories of childhood, of Mummy and of Mademoiselle Rosen, came flooding back.

They had lived together, Mummy and she, in a solid house that grandfather had had built after the First World War, in what had then been the genteel outskirts of a Midlands industrial city, but which had long since been intruded upon by a belt of broad boulevards and raw council estates. Happily, St. Aubyn stood well back from the road, and if its rock-gardened heights gave a view of the cut-price corner shop opposite, the lower privet hedge prevented folks on the near pavement from looking up at the lace-curtained windows.

Mummy was very beautiful: pale-skinned and blue-eyed; always carrying the scent of toilet soap and lavender water; small-boned like a bird; so soft-smelling and lovely that Candida often ached to wrap her thin arms about the slim waist and nuzzle against the frills at her throat and bosom. Sometimes she did this, and Mummy would be indulgent for a little while—before she gently disentangled herself with a mild reproof: "Now, darling, we mustn't have too much of these silly goings-on, must we?"

They were comfortably off. Mummy had a good widow's pension from the County Council, supplemented by a legacy from a late, well-to-do aunt. Candida went to a small private school for girls that was only five minutes cycle ride from St. Aubyn. Mummy always watched from the front gate till she was out of sight, and she was told never to stop for anyone, particularly strange men who might offer her sweets.

Mademoiselle Rosen entered her life in the summer term of her eleventh year, when the Frenchwoman came to the school under an exchange scheme. No one would have thought of hugging Helene Rosen; she was tall and thin, with a muddy skin and dull eyes behind thick glasses. It was she who discovered that Candida had a good memory and a natural ear for accent. By the following spring, fired by her teacher's encouragement, Candida had reached the third volume of the school's standard French textbook—and earned a private prize: a copy of *Lettres de mon Moulin*, inscribed "*à ma meilleure élève, de Hélène Rosen*"—while the rest of the form were still struggling through Book One.

Then followed private lessons at Mlle. Rosen's lodgings every Tuesday and Thursday. Mummy had been doubtful about this arrangement. She said: "Candida works much too hard as it is, and I'm sure she's outgrowing her strength. That's why she's always so peaky and anemic-looking."

It was Uncle Bernard who talked her round: he was Mummy's oldest friend, who always fell asleep in front of television and lost every time at Monopoly.

Mlle. Rosen reluctantly accepted the half guinea a week that Mummy offered her for the lessons—and lavished it on fancy cakes, tinned fruit, or fresh strawberries in season, for her young pupil's tea before lessons began.

Mummy decided she must ask "that poor young woman"

round for a little light supper, to get to know her better. Mlle. Rosen arrived in a grubby lace dress that won a raised eyebrow from her hostess.

Candida—in bed as usual by eight-thirty—was aroused by the sound of a door slamming downstairs and by Mummy's voice raised in anger. She crept out of bed and crouched at the top of the stairwell, to hear Mlle. Rosen crying and Mummy saying, in a calm and reasonable tone of voice: "I think you'd better go, mademoiselle—and I'd be most grateful if you don't see my daughter more than is necessary in the future."

That was the end of the private lessons. From then on, Mlle. Rosen treated her like all the other girls in the form; no, differently—for she never looked directly at her. But, sometimes Candida caught her stolen glance and was disturbed by the expression—instantly quenched—in those dull eyes.

It was many months later—and Mlle. Rosen had long since returned to France—that she heard the truth about that night of the little light supper.

"Sonia couldn't wait," said Hilary Lubbock. "She wanted to get to the hotel and hang up dresses and things. She's quite cut up about you, of course, and felt she should have stayed, but—well, you know Sonia—she's a great one for duty."

Haquin had provided them with a plain car and a lounge-suited driver, and they had joined the late afternoon traffic in the Quai des Tuileries. The rain had stopped, and all Paris was overlaid with a patchwork quilt of sunlight and shadow.

"It was nice of you to stay," said Candida, wondering why he seemed to find it necessary to apologize for Sonia Hammersley.

"She also wanted to put through a quiet call to Grave Vale," he said. "They have to be warned about what's happened before the rest of the press get hold of it—though Superintendent Haquin says the police here won't be releasing the story. Not yet."

She concentrated on looking out of the window, across the flecked blue of the river, to a spot in the draggle-tailed clouds above the Eiffel Tower where a southbound airliner was tracing a pencil line of whiteness. When she shuddered, his big hand immediately closed over hers, which meant that he had been covertly watching her.

She quite liked Hilary Lubbock, for there was nothing about him to dislike. He was everybody's friend: a big, healthy, undemanding dog of a man who surprisingly produced quite imaginative and perceptive photographs.

They had worked together several times, and had slipped into the easy camaraderie that often exists between professionals of opposite sexes when there is no personal involvement.

But that hand—neutral-cool, dry and disquieting—had to be got rid of. She turned her mind to the prospect of removing her own, on some pretext like touching her hair, as soon as possible.

"Don't let it get you down, ducks," he said. "Sure, it was a ghastly thing to have happened—and to you, of all people —but it's all over now. The fuzz will straighten it out. It was obviously those damn' student yobs at the airport bar. We all think so, and Haquin agrees."

She wasn't able to answer, but looked down at his hand, which he immediately drew away. He was making a protracted business of lighting a cigarette as their driver slotted into the lines of traffic that circled the Place de la Concorde.

It was a relief to reach the hotel, which was a familiar

Paris home during the Collections, when it was filled with models, photographers and magazine people: faces she saw every day of her working life. A porter took their cases (Haquin had kept the hatbox, but had provided a carrier bag for her bits and pieces), and they passed in through the plate-glass doors. There were no familiar faces: only middle-aged and elderly tourists, plastic-macked and camera-hung, waiting for transport. She bowed her eyes and followed behind Hilary Lubbock, past the reflective stares of well-barbered Americans and their expensively preserved consorts, to the reception desk.

"Miss Jeans and Mr. Lubbock—rooms forty-six and forty-nine."

It was a new reception clerk, and not the usual one, who passed over their keys.

"Is there a letter for me, please?" asked Candida.

He checked the pigeonhole. "No, Miss Jeans."

"Will there be another delivery today?"

"Not till tomorrow morning, Miss Jeans."

Candida murmured something noncommittal and joined Lubbock in the rickety little lift. She saw the reflection of her troubled eyes watching her over the slope of her companion's shoulder, and the confines of the narrow compartment dictated that they must stand face to face, so her expression was naked to his regard.

"Sonia wants us all to go out to dinner together," he said, "but it will be all of three hours before she starts making hungry noises. Why not have a nice hot bath and a kip? I know I shall."

She nodded. They were moving very slowly up to the fourth floor, where their rooms were, and every nerve ending of her body shrank from the expectation that he might touch her.

"You do just that. And, Candy . . ."

"Yes?" Guardedly. This could be the moment where he might very well slide his fingers round the upper part of her arm, or take her chin in his hand. But he didn't.

"Tell me it's none of my business, but I know something's troubling you. It was obvious when we met this morning. And what happened at the airport must have come as a ghastly side swipe . . ."—his face, very close to hers, was beefy, bland and speckled with faint stubble around the mouth and chin—". . . so I'd like you to know that I'm basically a brotherly shoulder to cry on."

"Thanks, Hilary." She cast an agonized glance, to see the third floor sliding slowly past.

He grinned boyishly and struck a posture, slapping his shoulder.

"Now. All together—what am I?"

She laughed, despite herself.

"A brotherly shoulder to cry on."

"Well done, ducks."

He hugged her antiseptically, and the lift glided to a halt.

They parted in the corridor, with a thickly carpeted floor that creaked underfoot; quite good pieces of Third Empire furniture and ferns in faience vases. Lubbock indeed looked very brotherly and innocuous in the dim light.

"See ya. I'll give you a ring about seven," he said. "And remember what I said, won't you?"

She kept a tight smile till the door was closed behind her, then she leaned back against it and closed her eyes in misery.

"He didn't write the letter," she said aloud. "Jeremy didn't write. I knew he wouldn't. . . ."

She had met Jeremy Stanton at a party to which she had been taken by a photographer—not Hilary Lubbock—who had kept her working late: her escort squared his conscience by simply easing her into the scented jostle, fixing her with a drink, then going off to find his boyfriend.

"I'm Mrs. Stanton's boy. I think she used to take in your mum's washing, and I've always wanted to meet you."

He caught her by the elbow, just as she had laid down her untasted drink on a side table and was tactfully sliding toward the door. She knew him from magazine credit lines, from occasional TV appearances and from the chit-chat of models' dressing rooms, where the mention of his name was always greeted by a certain amount of eyebrow-raising—from which Candida had always inferred that he was a womanizer.

And yet it had been so easy to forget all that—and she with all her hang-ups. The palpably drunk Jeremy Stanton was like a little boy lost, peeling off his armor like onion skins and strewing them round her feet.

He had a heavy Mediterranean tan, and a jet-black forelock flopped over his brow. She had an impulse to smooth it back.

She let him propel her through the pot-smoking and mutually pawing couples, to the scented night air of a wrought-iron balcony overlooking delicately lit lime trees. And there they talked—or, rather, he talked and she listened —about all life, all art and Jeremy Stanton.

He came, he said, from a talented drinking family of abysmal introverts, which left him an eternal six whiskies below par: below what most people regarded as the normal level of human communication. Normal communication, for Jeremy Stanton plus six whiskies, he said, was a dazzling euphoria that made him want to shout for joy and kiss people; and wasn't that nice, when his habitual below-par state was one that made him either want to ride full tilt at humanity with a dripping saber, or hide away in a barrel? Euphoria was distinctly better.

Candida, leaning against sun-warmed brick, with night wind stirring the folds of her skirt, accepted his kiss by turning her cheek—and was surprised at its gentleness, which hardly squared with his dressing-room reputation.

He talked about sin with an affected hedonism that completely disarmed her. The word sin, in itself, seemed a curiously bland and archaic term. If he had said "sex" or "vice," she would have been embarrassed. Thoroughly to enjoy sinning, he said, you had to have been brought up a Catholic—as he had been—and cunningly conditioned by those splendid fellows, the Jesuits, into an awareness of the shape, size and consequences of your sins. These characters inside—he nodded contemptuously to the open window—were representatives of a civilization that had forgotten what it was all about: lured on by the beckoning carrot of self-indulgence, they sinned without fear and—because guiltless sin follows the law of diminishing returns—without pleasure.

With him, he said, it was quite different. As a lapsed Catholic, he knew that every unconfessed sin was being piled up in the balance against him, and every sin was fresh and culpable as the one that had gone before, so that there was no lessening of the fierce delight of living dangerously with —would you believe a million years in Hell—staked on every wrong act?

He laughed then: a full-throated, unaffected laugh that implied he had made an elaborate joke, to amuse her. And she found herself joining in.

That was the beginning. He didn't offer to see her home, which surprised her, but strode out into the scudding traffic and rode back on the running board of a taxi he'd managed to snatch. Another unexpectedly tender kiss—this time aimed directly at her cheek—and he went back to the party, leaving her bemused and intrigued.

In the days that followed, she thought a lot about Jeremy Stanton: telling herself that it was ridiculous still to be so conscious of her orphan-ness at the age of twenty-two; that it was time she stopped mourning the loss of Mummy, and tried a taste of the world outside.

A week later, she met Stanton during a photo session at the Grave Vale studios. He was shirt-sleeved, sober, and absorbed, and hardly took any notice of her till quitting time, when he asked her if she was free for dinner.

She was.

◀ THREE ▶

TUESDAY BEGAN BADLY. Sonia had ordered a taxi for nine-thirty: at ten o'clock, Candida and Lubbock were still waiting near the hotel's plate-glass doors, with the camera gear and a suitcase containing the changes of clothes. Candida—already dressed in one of the black ensembles: black suit, hat, gloves and umbrella—was only numbly aware of the curious and appraising stares she was getting from the people passing in and out of the foyer. Lubbock was spelling his way, painfully, through a copy of *Paris-Matin*. Sonia Hammersley was over at the reception desk, where the clerk was crumbling under the strain of her shrill invective and trying to phone through to the taxi rank.

Lubbock folded up the newspaper with a grunt. "As far as my blessed French is equal to the task," he said, "there doesn't appear to be anything in here about—you know."

Candida said nothing. She had managed, overnight, to squeeze the horror of the previous afternoon into a far corner of her mind, where it had been overlaid by a dull ache of disappointment. There had been no letter for her that morning, either.

"Little Sonia's giving that poor chap hell," said Lubbock. "Something's definitely upset our little Sonia. She was a bit snappy last night, too."

The previous evening, they had had dinner at a seafood restaurant on one of the *quais*. Sonia had been alternately sullen and rude, and Candida absorbed in her private miseries—while Lubbock had manfully carried on the burden of a limping monologue. Poor man, for having to cope with two neurotic women, thought Candida. He really is quite a nice person.

"I think this is it," he said, as an empty taxi drew up outside. "Yes, it is! . . . Sonia, love!"

Sonia threw the clerk a parting scowl and came running. She picked up the suitcase, forestalling Candida.

"Leave the damn' thing to me, and get into the car. You'll only split those gloves!"

Candida obeyed meekly, taking only the carrier bag that they had given her at the police station, containing her make-up and bits and pieces.

Lubbock instructed the driver. They were barely out of sight of the hotel before Sonia swore.

"What's up, ducks?" asked Lubbock.

"Damn! I meant to hire a black poodle for her to be carrying in this session. It would have been a terrific gimmick."

"Too late for that now," said Lubbock. "By the look of the sky, we'll be lucky to get any shooting in before the rain starts, as it is."

Candida dragged her mind to the here and now.

"They don't usually allow dogs in cemeteries," she ventured.

"They do in this one," said Sonia savagely. "It's a dogs' bloody cemetery!"

They passed through Clichy along a shabby boulevard sliced through a section of working-class Paris. Alive as an overturned anthill: a long street of cooked meat shops with salamis hung in fat swags; gilded rocking-horse heads, staring eyed, above *charcuteries;* gossiping housewives and hurrying priests in Basque berets; a line of white-faced children filing into a church that was set back from the road in a littered square lined with dead, grimed trees; *pâtisserie, boulangerie, meubles; laiterie, boucherie,* and *entrepreneur des pompes funèbres;* and a café on the corner of every block, where old men sucked their drinks, deaf to the charivari.

Out into an open space flanked by naked concrete tenements and bulldozed earth, they saw the chimneys and cylinders of a gasworks and the gray line of the river.

"There's no place around here for a cemetery," snapped Sonia Hammersley. "Have we come the wrong way?"

"It is on an island in the middle of the river, madame," said the driver mildly.

They stopped halfway across the bridge, and there was a flaking stucco wall opposite, with wrought-iron gates and a faded notice:

La Cimetière des Chiens
Prix d'entrer 2f.

Lubbock paid off the taxi, and they crossed through the lines of honking traffic. Unaccountably, two policemen seemed to be guarding the cemetery gate, and Candida shrank when one of them snapped her a smiling salute.

They were on a small hump-backed island bisected by the bridge: a bijou place of rustling trees and narrow dirt paths. Facing them was a shabby reception building and some kind of monument. Beyond that, they could see packed rows of tiny gravestones, and a few solitary-looking people. Below, the river sluiced swiftly past, half-hidden by screens of bushes.

"We'd better get a move on before the rain starts," said Lubbock, and he started to unpack his gear.

Sonia went over to the window of the reception building, and Candida walked closer to the monument. It stood on a small knoll and carried a crude carving of a large dog with a child lying astride its back, set against a rugged backdrop that was intended to resemble alpine heights, with chalets on the crest. There was a carved scroll beneath.

" 'Barry the St. Bernard,' " translated Candida aloud. " 'He saved forty persons' lives and was killed by the forty-first.' Poor Barry. How unkind."

She heard the snap of a Hasselblad's shutter, and automatically tilted her chin. Snap—pause—snap. She swung round to face the other way, slid one foot forward, and extended both her gloved hands onto the crook of the umbrella.

"Lovely, duckie, lovely. Let's have that one again. A bit more pensive-looking. Pout a bit. Yes—hold it! Fine!"

Hilary Lubbock at work was strong and demanding. He circled around her, hunched over his camera, cajoling her constantly, bullying and flattering.

Now, her mind was washed clear of everything but the familiar *rapport* that had been triggered off by the first sound of his shutter. Now, she was a trained doll: a living but impersonal manikin whose only purpose was to make images on the strip of film that was passing behind the iris of the camera's eye. Not Candida Jeans any longer, but a

face and figure in the current mode, destined for a brief
life-span in the expensive glossies.

Sonia rejoined them. She teased out a curl against
Candida's cheek, and brushed away a fleck of lint from the
shoulder of the black suit. Now, she was all professional,
and her particular private malaise put aside in wraps.

"Thank heaven something's going right with this trip," she
said. "They got my letter, and know all about us. We can
do practically anything we like, provided we don't stand on
the gravestones, and they've made a sort of cubbyhole with
a screen in the corner of the office. It isn't much, but you'll
have room to change. Do you think we should move on to
another spot, Hilary?"

"I'll finish off this roll," said Lubbock. "The rain's nearly
on us."

It came almost immediately after that: a fine drizzle from
the slate-gray overcast that now hid the upper halves of the
gasworks chimneys across the river. It lay on the nap of the
black suit in a million pinpoints of diamond.

"The light's terrific," said Lubbock. "Let her get wet, or
maybe some business with the raised umbrella, perhaps."

"Not on Day One," said Sonia. "This material goes like all
hell after a wetting. We'll do the black plastic mack and
boots. Go and get changed, Candida. You'll have to cope on
your own, there's not room for the two of us."

They sold postcards and china souvenirs of Barry's grave
inside the stuffy office, and there was a scent of dried garlic
flowers. A middle-aged woman in spectacles was behind the
reception counter. She looked up from writing something,
and pointed Candida toward a baize-covered screen set in a
far corner of the small room, then went back to what she
was doing. An elderly couple in black were following the
course of her slowly-moving pen with lugubrious eyes.

"The name of the deceased?" asked the woman behind the counter.

"Jo-jo."

"Sex of the deceased?"

"Male."

Candida squeezed in behind the screen, the inside of which was stuck all over with St. Raphael and Cinzano posters. The suitcase was open on the floor, and her bits and pieces carrier stood on a chair. To her relief, there was a hanging mirror—large, if flyblown. She slid out of the jacket and hung it carefully on a hanger.

"Now, do monsieur and madame wish to take advantage of guaranteed perpetual interment for their little friend, or do they wish to have the annual tenure?"

"Er—how much is that, the perpetual interment?"

Out of the skirt and into shiny culottes. The high boots pinched abominably, but she wouldn't be doing much walking. Face and hair first, then the mack—which was sure to be tight under the arms.

"Does that include looking after the grave, madame?"

"After we've gone, he means. Heaven knows, we shall continue to come and keep poor Jo-jo tidy while ever we have the strength to take the bus from Vincennes."

"But of course, monsieur. Do you see an untidy grave in the cemetery, even among the oldest interments?"

"I'm sure it's all very nice."

"There is true reverence here, madame."

She lifted a silk square from the top of the carrier bag and dabbed the remains of the rain from her hair, to prevent it from going lank under the comb. Comb—where was the comb? Everything seems to have been turned upside down in the carrier. . . .

"Regarding the tombstone . . ."

"This is entirely up to monsieur and madame, with due regard for the regulations of the cemetery in matters of good taste. I can give monsieur and madame the addresses of two local stonemasons who . . ."

The breathy scream sent the pen skittering from the woman's fingers and across the counter. The three of them turned, shocked to silence, as Candida fought her way from behind the screen and clung, sobbing, to a revolving postcard stand.

"Mademoiselle! Have you taken leave of your senses?" It was the woman behind the counter who was the first to find her voice. "What is the matter with you?"

The old couple fixed their bovine stares on the half-naked, booted girl. The man took out a handkerchief and slowly wiped his rheumy eyes.

"Mademoiselle! I must protest! This is a place of sorrow and mourning!" She came out from behind the counter and took Candida firmly by the arm. "Go out of sight at once, and cover yourself."

Candida slide her gaze from the colored postcards to the woman's pinched, pink face. Through her terror, a small voice was crying out to her from the end of an illimitable corridor, warning her to be careful.

"I—I'm sorry," she said, cupping her breasts in her hands.

"So you should be, mademoiselle. Now, get out of sight, I beg you, before anyone else comes in. In all my years of employment in this cemetery, this has never happened before."

"I felt—suddenly ill," said Candida.

"A cemetery is not a place to be ill," said the woman implacably. "If this continues, I shall have to call the patron and have you and your people removed."

Candida shrugged her way behind the screen and out of

their sight, eyes closed, trembling. She stood for a while, huddling the upper part of her body with her arms, touching the raised ridges of gooseflesh on her bare skin; till the far-off, warning voice told her that she had been a long time, and that an irascible Sonia Hammersley would soon come elbowing her way behind the screen, with a sarcastic remark that would choke to silence in her throat when she saw— *that*.

She forced herself to look. The carrier bag was where she had dropped it a few moments before, with the pile of bits and pieces that she had emptied out onto the floor, to sort out: make-up, hair-piece, comb and brush, a bundle of orange sticks fastened with an elastic band, a box of tissues. . . .

And the obscene thing that poked out from under the carrier bag, still half-wrapped in paper that was dabbled with dried blotches of watery blood: four white fingers and a white thumb, splayed like the legs of a crouching spider.

"This is a delicate matter, monsieur and madame, but do you wish the remains of your little friend to be embalmed?"

"Oh! I can't bear to think about it!"

"There, there, Hortense! Calm yourself. What would old Jo-jo think if he could see his dear mistress carrying on like that, eh?"

A long barge swept swiftly past, carried on the Seine flood, loaded down to the rubbing strake with cement. A man in a pom-pom hat at the tiller took his pipe from his mouth and waved it to them. A woman came out of the cabin door and emptied a basin of slops over the side. A terrier dog strutted, stiff-legged and proprietorial, the length of the rusty iron deck. A grimy Dutch tricolor flapped at the stern, where screeching seagulls swooped for scraps.

"I wish to God this rain would stop," said Sonia Hammersley.

"We're doing fine," said Lubbock. "This grayness is just
right for the setting. Who needs sunshine and blue skies?
Just wait till you see the pictures, duckie. You'll flip. Head
down a bit, Candy—that's right—make like you're arrang-
ing the flowers on dear old Fido's grave. Lovely! Moisten
your lips again. Lovely!"

The flowers were *eternelles*, crisp as small shards of bone
between her fingers, and they lay on a slab of veined, black
marble. The inscription was incised and gilded:

JACKY
18 ème September 1965
Adieu, petit ami

Calm. No matter what, she had to stay calm. . . .

Somehow—using a wadded bundle of tissues and closing
her eyes—she had forced herself to pick the thing up and
drop it into the bottom of the carrier bag. It lay there now,
covered by the empty tissue box, with all the other things
on top.

But—what to do next?

Think, girl. Think. . . .

"All right, we'll try another spot. What about the lower
level, Sonia? With a tombstone in the foreground and Candy
silhouetted against the river, eh?"

"If you like. Oh, for heaven's sake, girl, your belt's
twisted at the back. Can't you even dress yourself properly?"

"I'm sorry, Sonia."

The principal part of the pets' cemetery—there were cats
as well as dogs buried there—lay along the spine of the
narrow island, where the small tombstones were packed in

close rows along several narrow paths. There they had come across about half-a-dozen people visiting, or tending, the pathetic testaments to their devotion; and Hilary Lubbock had taken time off to shoot some pictures of a bourgeois young couple and their small son; kneeling under a dripping laurel bush, to get them standing about the grave of a dog called Nana, the menfolk bareheaded and all three of them disregarding the intrusion upon their private grief.

Now Lubbock was leading the way down an inclined path that led to the shoreline of the small island, where the graves seemed poorer and more exiguous. There was an old woman with a black shawl over her head, bowed over a small hummock of bare earth, on which was set a jam jar with some tired-looking violets.

Candida was photographed with her: the two of them standing side by side, with the old woman plucking at Candida's sleeve. Her face was grimed in the wrinkles and she was nearly bald under the shawl.

"How pretty you are, mam'selle," she mumbled. "Get all the men running after what you've got to offer, I shouldn't wonder." She prodded Candida and laughed obscenely.

"Show a bit of animation, Candy," called Lubbock. "Talk to the old duck. You're supposed to speak French like a native. And keep your chin up, love."

Candida mouthed something. . . .

One thing was certain: she must keep calm. Yesterday's horror was something from which it had been quite easy to disassociate; the shock of it had sent her into a shuddering heap, but it had been a random blow struck from the outside, a students' hideous prank, something for which she had been in no way responsible—something for the police alone.

That was the way it *had* been; now the whole world had gone mad. The random blow from the outside had suddenly become a private horror of her own. From inside.

Who in the whole wide world—including Sonia Hammersley and Hilary Lubbock, not to mention the grave-faced policeman with the limp—would ever believe that she, Candida Jeans, was in no way responsible for the double horror?

"All right, Candy—relax!" called Lubbock.

"He's your style," said the old woman. "Limbs like a dray horse. But you'll not need me to tell you that, eh?"

"All right, ma," said Lubbock. "The show's over." He appealed to Candida: "Love, tell the old bag we don't want any more pictures."

The old woman searched Candida's face. "Is that all, then? There'll be some drink money in it for me, won't there, dearie?"

Candida squirmed out of the woman's grasp, and went over to a wooden railing that lined the edge of the path. A pair of mute swans were battling their way upriver, breasting and bobbing against the current.

"Give her some money, Hilary," she said.

"How much?"

"A couple of francs will do."

Only one answer: the thing that lay at the bottom of the carrier bag behind the screen in the reception office had to be pushed out of her life.

But how—and where?

"What I need," said Sonia Hammersley firmly, "is a drink before lunch. Let's pack up, get a cab, and drive away from this ghastly neck of the woods, to a civilized bar in the Champs Élysées."

"I'll second that," said Lubbock.

Continuous streams of traffic poured across the bridge from both directions, tires hissing on the wet *pavé*—but there was not a free taxi in sight.

"You're a man—*do* something!" rasped Sonia Hammersley.
Lubbock stole a wink at Candida and picked up the suitcase.

"This man's going to walk till he finds a taxi rank."
They found a taxi rank on a corner three blocks down the
boulevard, signaled by a queue of people standing like patient
cattle in the new downpour. Most of them were ladened
with shopping bags: it was Tuesday, and there were market
stalls in all the side streets.

"What now?" said Sonia Hammersley. "Can't we catch a
bus or something—or the Metro?"

"The buses are so full you'd have to sit on the roof," said
Lubbock, "and there's no Metro station nearer than the Porte
de Clichy. What we'll do is wait in here till the taxi queue
thins out a bit at lunch time."

"Here" was a small café on the corner opposite the taxi
rank: a brass-topped bar and banks of colorful bottles;
shirt-sleeved proprietor with a half-smoked Gauloise stuck
behind his ear; a monkey-faced little waiter in a soiled white
jacket; the popping of a pin-table machine; a sea of cloth-
capped heads that turned to regard them.

"I'm not going in a joint like that!" hissed Sonia
Hammersley.

"Stay wet and thirsty then, ducks," said Lubbock. "Come
on, Candy."

The two girls followed him in, and the big Englishman
won a comradely grin from the proprietor when he effort-
lessly hefted the suitcase onto the bar counter.

"'sokay, sair. I look after it."

"Give him your carrier bag, Candy."

"I–I think I'll keep it with me," said Candy hastily.

But the bulky carrier bag became an impediment as soon

as they began to edge their way toward an empty table by the window; a Clichy workman swore when she dislodged his cap, but changed it to a growl of appreciation when he saw her back view.

Their table was tucked closely into the curve of the window at the corner, not more than ten paces from the taxi queue. Candida laid the carrier bag by the side of her leg, and concentrated on trying to forget it was there. But it wouldn't work.

"What's it to be, then, gels?" said Lubbock. The diminutive waiter was hovering close to Candida's elbow.

Sonia Hammersley demanded whisky and ginger ale, Lubbock plumped for a white *vin ordinaire*, Candida thought she would have a coffee. Then Sonia went to find the loo.

"Are you all right, Candy?" asked Lubbock, when they were alone. "You look like death."

"I'm all right, Hilary."

"Not still shaken up about what happened yesterday—or brooding over your own private worry, whatever it is?"

"No."

"La belle Sonia getting you down? She is me. Cripes! I've worked with her before, but it was never like this. I don't know what's eating her, but I do know this: I'll starve on the Embankment or send my old mum out into the streets to keep me before I come away on another job with her. Watch your elbow, love, here comes the cupbearer."

The waiter took Canadida's *café filtre* from his heavily ladened tray and slid it in front of her; moved a sideways pace toward Lubbock—and tripped over the carrier bag.

There was the shattering of glass and china, and the cymbal clash of the metal tray. Every head flicked round.

Silence—save for a ball in the pin-table that continued to cannon its way down noisily, from obstacle to obstacle. Candida made an anguished snatch at the overturned carrier and lifted it onto her lap.

The rest was a nightmare of angry Gallic faces, shrill accusations and pointing fingers, as the proprietor and his wife joined the very shaken waiter. Candida willed herself into a limbo, huddling the hateful carrier with both arms. Somewhere on the edge of her consciousness, she was aware that Sonia Hammersley had rejoined them and was adding her own brand of scorn and derision to theirs. She had a wild impulse to leap up and run out of the café, or to break out of the window, and hide herself and her guilty burden in a dark, quiet corner of the teeming city.

Then she felt it: a cold trickle of wetness on her thighs.

Sliding a hand under the carrier bag, she felt her fingers bore holes in sodden pulp.

The brown paper bag had stood, for a few seconds, in the widening lake of spilled drinks that the proprietor's wife was now swabbing up, complainingly, with a mop. And now the bottom was falling out!

Her trembling fingers quested further. She felt the lower layer of damp, balled-up tissues. Then something soft, chill and lumpish: the severed hand.

With a despairing moan, she gathered the bag in her arms and pressed it to her.

"A complete accident," said Hilary Lubbock. "The lady didn't notice that the bag had fallen over on its side, and the waiter couldn't help falling over it."

"Try it on them in French," sneered Sonia Hammersley.

But the atmosphere was changing. One of the workmen at the next table was joshing the waiter, elbowing him in the thigh and making some crudely appreciative comment about the girl in the shiny mack and boots; the waiter grinned sheepishly and rubbed his bruised knee. The proprietor's wife had wiped up the mess; she was loudly offering the mixed slops in her bucket at twenty-five centimes a glass. The incident had had a buoyant effect on the wet Tuesday workaday life of the café.

Lubbock settled the matter by sliding a twenty-franc note to the proprietor. The fellow took it with a salute and went back to the bar. He came back a few minutes later with a white plastic shopping bag, the sort they provide at supermarkets.

Candida looked up to see him looming over her.

"Slip your bits and pieces bag in that," said Lubbock.

"For God's sake, girl, he's trying to help you," said Sonia Hammersley. "Get rid of the wretched thing. Let him put it with the suitcase before we have another ghastly scene."

She herself slid the ruined carrier bag into the envelope of substantial plastic, and felt the contents thud against the base as the sodden brown paper gave way. She made no protest when he took it away from her; but watched him carry it behind the bar and lay it somewhere out of sight.

"That old taxi queue doesn't get any less," said Lubbock. "I propose we abandon all hope of a proper lunch and settle for a snack here. Then we grab the first available cab and go straight on to the next job. What do you say, Candy?"

"No good talking to *her*," said Sonia Hammersley. "She's not with us."

Let time go by quickly. There was the whole wilderness of the long afternoon to face, but at the end of it there would be the blessed moment when she was able to shut out the whole world behind the door of her hotel room.

And there—alone and secretly—she would be able to think out how to rid herself of the horror that had attached itself to her.

"Well, if you chicks aren't hungry," said Lubbock. "I am. And I think I'm going to settle for yer actual *jambon sandwich Français*."

◀ FOUR ▶

ALL PARIS FURLED its umbrella in the late afternoon, when
the overcast cleared away to the east, and the rain with it.
Busy waiters laid out the tables and chairs outside the cafés
in the great boulevards, and the sun-blinds came down. In
the garden of the Tuileries, the white sails of toy yachts
slanted across the round pond in the lazy wind. Lovers held
hands in quiet corners of grassy squares. Starlings sang again
in the lime trees.

Candida modeled in the sunlight of a stonemason's yard in
Montparnasse, her eyes—and her thoughts—hidden behind
outsized dark glasses. She wandered, like a slim wraith in
swirling black chiffon, among the tumbled heaps of shaped
marble and limestone; touching the carved wings of fallen
angels; trailing her fingers down ivy-girt columns; laying
her cheek against the cold lips of a sculptured saint. Hilary
Lubbock followed her, shooting from every angle.

"This is fantastic," he said. "Fantastic. You could build your feature on these pictures alone."

Sonia Hammersley didn't think the session was all that hot, and said so. She had had three more large whiskies at the café in Clichy, and her aggression had given way to a stubborn sourness. The setting was all wrong. Who wanted to see a background of brick wall? They never should have come here in the first place. Candida had better change into the slacks and shirt and do the whole thing over again. Reshoot the chiffon in tomorrow's session.

"Have a heart, love," protested Lubbock. "It's nearly five o'clock. I'm squint-eyed from peering through this blessed viewfinder, and Candy's visibly wilting."

But Sonia was the boss; the end of the long arm of the power and majesty of Grave Vale Press, who were footing the bill. So Candida had to go through the whole routine again, in a different rig-out. It was past six o'clock before they had done; the workmen had gone long since, and the foreman of the yard was meaningfully jangling his keys near the gate.

The foreman watched them pack the clothes into the suitcase, and lost his sourness when Lubbock gave him five francs. He grinned amiably at Candida as she followed the others through the gate.

"Don't take our old cat with you, mam'selle," he said. "She's been sniffing round that bag of yours for the last half-hour. I don't know what you've got in there, but that greedy-guts will follow you across Paris for it."

Candida stiffened with horror when she saw a black-and-white cat crouched beside her, its questing nostrils raised toward the bottom of the plastic bag.

The foreman gathered up the cat in one hand and shut

the gate, shaking his head in puzzlement to see the girl in black racing down the road ahead of her companions.

The lights were off in her room and the blinds drawn. What she had to do—the nerve-searing and necessary task of enclosing the horror in a small and innocent-looking package— was not to be borne in full view. With only the chinks of dying daylight from the edge of the curtains, and with her eyes half-turned away, she lifted the thing out of its bed of damp, mashed tissues with the ends of two coat hangers, dropped it into an empty shoebox and clamped down the lid.

She sat back on her heels and listened to the pounding of a vein in her head.

Think. . . .

It was nearly dark, and she'd excused herself from going out to dinner with the others on the pretext of a migraine. Let another half an hour go by, then pick up the box and go down by the stairs—out into the busy, anonymous streets.

The shoebox stood out whitely against the dark-colored carpet, dominating the gloom. She got up and snapped on the room lights, all of them. When she went over to the hand-basin, she made a wide detour round the box.

Her haunted eyes stared out at her from the mirror as she felt the touch of water on her soiled hands.

Cleanliness, Mummy always said, was next to godliness. Soiled or untidily arranged things were anathema to her; she was unable to get her tongue round the word "dirt" without wrinkling her nose.

A short-haired cat, that didn't moult all over the sofas and chairs, was a soft and desirable creature to have around the house, because cats are able to look after themselves

decently. But even the succession of cleanly St. Aubyn cats—
who were all named "Wissie"—needed attention after they
had been out. "Wissie wants to come in, darling. Make him
nice." This meant wiping each velvety pad with first a damp
and then a dry cloth.

If Mummy reminded Candida of an infinitely more fastid-
ious Wissie, Uncle Bernard, being male, related more nearly
to the canine: a big man with a deep voice and rough-
textured suits. But he had a pleasant, spicy smell of gentle-
men's shaving lotion, and the scalp that showed through
the crown of his sandy hair was pink and scrubbed-looking.
There was a pair of Daddy's old carpet slippers waiting by
the umbrella stand near the front door, for when Uncle
Bernard came to call. Whenever he felt like a pipe, he always
went out into the garden.

Daddy had been a member of Uncle Bernard's Masonic
Lodge. Uncle Bernard came at least one evening a week,
and always for Sunday lunch. He was a widower who had
sold up and retired early from a prosperous wholesale grocery
business in the city. With no close family but a grown-up
son in Australia, he had so become a part of the enclosed
life at St. Aubyn that Candida could not remember a time
when the toot of his car horn in the steep slope of the
drive had not meant chocolates or a plaything for her. With
no recollection of Daddy—who had passed away when she
was a baby—Uncle Bernard filled a certain gap in her upbringing. On fine Sunday mornings they played together in
the garden behind the house—a plateau of neat grass shaded
by a hollow square of whispering cypress trees—till Mummy
called them in from the game of French cricket, I-Spy or
Blind-Man's Buff.

"Lunch time, you two. Change into slippers and wash
hands."

Early evenings meant watching children's television—which Mummy also enjoyed—and the community hymn singing on Sundays. After that, the set was firmly switched off for a threesome game of Monopoly, at which Uncle Bernard always played with a disregard for the laws of probability that landed him with more undeveloped properties than anyone else, but with no capital in hand to pay off even the smallest debt without having to mortgage something at a loss. He usually went broke and sat out the last half of the game, nodding over the cat on his knees, while the others fought to a keen finish that invariably turned upon whether the fall of the dice landed Mummy on one of Candida's two expensive hotels in the luxury district before Candida came unstuck on several of Mummy's modest-sized housing estates in the solid bourgeois areas.

The evening Candida learned the truth about the Mlle. Rosen episode was like any other Sunday, except that there was one of those impending world crises that threatened to lead to a holocaust which could even swallow up the cosy living room at St. Aubyn.

Mummy was counting out some rent to pay, when Uncle Bernard woke up, glanced at his watch and said: "I think we should look in at the news and see how things are, Edith."

"Yes," said Mummy. And then—tight-mouthed after checking the time: "It's only five minutes to, and we don't want to be subjected to the end of one of their disgusting plays, or the sight of some shameless women kicking their legs." Mummy was a member of a nationwide movement to clean up the television medium.

On the hour—and Candida only avoided being sent to bed by pleading that she was close to winning the Monopoly—the picture flickered up to reveal the two opposing foreign secretaries smiling falsely and shaking hands. The crisis had

collapsed in a compromise: all humanity—and St. Aubyn—
was safe again till the next time.

The announcer's voice slipped smoothly from portentous-
ness to reverence, and Mummy's hand was stayed from the
act of switching off by a close-up of the Archbishop of
Canterbury, who had a comment to make upon mankind's
timely deliverance. She left the set on, and went back to
her seat. But not for long. The Primate's brief utterance
was followed by a kaleidoscope of short scenes from all over
a reprieved and jubilant world: waving crowds in the Champs
Élysées and before Buckingham Palace; grins and handclasps
at the White House; a close-up of sheepish tank crewmen
garlanded with flowers and kissed by pretty girls—it was
this scene that sent Mummy back to the set again.

But her hand on the knob was not quick enough to ex-
tinguish a zoomed-in shot of a crowd of teen-agers milling
round one of the spraying fountains in Trafalgar Square.
Candida saw it all: the unbelievable and incomprehensible
becoming hard, flat fact: the sight of a young girl being
carried, laughing, to the edge of the fountain—and the flash
of rubbery buttocks as she was hurled, naked, into the spray.

Snap . . .

"Disgusting! A war would have been better than that!"

Uncle Bernard said nothing, but applied himself to stroking
the underside of Wissie's chin with a crooked forefinger.
When Candida dared to slide her gaze, by easy stages, to
Mummy's face, it was in profile, pink and pinched about
the mouth. "Get your supper in the kitchen, Candida," she
said breathily. "There's fish-paste sandwiches between two
plates. Wash up the things afterwards, then go straight to
bed. I'll put away the game."

Candida kissed Mummy's flushed cheek and said good
night to Uncle Bernard. While eating her supper, she heard

them talking together in the next room. Mummy's voice was pitched higher than usual, counterpointed to the man's placatory baritone bumble.

She thought she heard her own name mentioned as she tiptoed up the stairs: it was this, as much as a questing desire to hear Mummy's reaction to the unbelievable thing that girl had allowed to happen to her on television, that brought her to the top of the stairwell an hour later.

She heard it all quite clearly. . . .

"I'm sure you're right, Edith. You usually are. But . . ."

"There's bad blood in the child, Bernard. The taint of heredity, and I thank God my hands are clean of it."

"I'm sure you do everything in your power to protect her."

"I do indeed. No one could do more. Bring her up to be modest about herself. Decent. To keep herself to herself. But—well—there was that French creature. Plain as a pike-staff. You'd have thought butter couldn't melt in her mouth, the two-faced creature."

"I understood there was a bit of unpleasantness. . . ."

"I caught her in the act. Oh, you don't know how difficult it is to talk about, even to you, an old friend. Well—I went out to the kitchen and when I came back into the sitting room that woman was *kissing* the photograph of Candida on the sideboard—*slobbering* over it. She'd taken off her glasses to do it. Well, you can imagine my feelings. . . ."

"She must have been—one of that sort, eh?"

"You can imagine my feelings, Bernard. There was no telling what had been going on. And, I mean—well—a woman like that would hardly have risked her job and everything. If she'd attempted anything nasty with an ordinary child, the girl would have reported her."

"You mean?"

"I had to face up to it. I thought it then, and I think it still. Candida must have encouraged the woman—led her on."

"Oh, I don't . . ."

"Yes, Bernard. It's in the blood. She inherits it from her father. Dirt. I do the best for her that I can, but how's she going to end up when I've gone? Like that brazen hussy on the television? . . ."

It was after that, red-eyed and choking, that Candida had stood for a long while at the wash basin in her darkened bedroom, with the cold tap gushing, symbolically, over her trembling hands.

Just a hurrying girl in a fawn coat and navy-blue slacks, carrying a shoebox; yet it seemed to her that she must be as conspicuous as a nude creature in a chariot trailing fire across the night sky. Men smiled at her when she passed them, and there was no concealment in the pitiless floodlights reflected from the Ionic bulk of the Madeleine, nor from the lit-up windows of the elegant shops on her right. She cut the far corner of the square, running out between the lines of speeding cars, deaf to the curses and the squealing tires; reached the top of the Rue Royale and saw the distant red tail-lights of the traffic circling the Place de la Concorde.

Beyond there, the all-concealing river ran darkly beneath the bridge from which she was going to drop her loathsome burden. All that was needed was to reach the bridge, then she would be free.

She passed a café, close by the front row of tables, where the apéritif drinkers were giving every passing face and figure their best attention. A middle-aged man in a curly-brimmed hat thought she had possibilities; dropped a handful of loose change beside his empty glass and came after her. He touched her elbow while she was waiting for a chance to cross between a gap in the passing traffic; the meaning of his politely phrased obscenities was almost lost on her; she broke away and ran blindly toward the center island. The traffic closed behind her and shut him off.

She paused, sucking in breath, splattered with fine spray from the illuminated waters of the fountain, staring ahead at the way she had to go; before she reached the bridge, she knew that she had made a bad mistake.

The bridge was crowded with strollers, for a start; moreover, they were bathed in the headlight beams of the endless streams of speeding cars, and pitilessly lit by overhead lamps. She walked past the gesticulating group of statuary guarding the end of the bridge, keeping close to the balustrade. Toward the middle, she paused for a few moments and looked down at the water. A boy and girl stopped close by her, hand in hand. There was a thud of engines, and a *bateau-mouche* slid directly beneath her; through the transparent roof of its dining saloon she could see white napery and the bare shoulders of women.

All the lights of Paris would have to be quenched; only then could she open the box and drop its loathsome contents.

Wearily, she turned back the way she had come.

To her left was the glaring white sweep of the Champs Élysées: no concealment there. But the bordering parkland offered promise, for it was lit only sparsely by strings of old-fashioned lampposts, and the flowering chestnut trees made dark patches on the grass and paths.

A group of youths detached themselves from a wrought-iron park bench and came after her, whistling at her and calling out assumed endearments. She panicked and ran. They came whooping after her. She ran till her heel turned and catapulted her headlong. The box went out of her hand and landed close by a substantial pair of black boots a yard from her extended hand.

"Are you all right, mam'selle?"

It was a caped policeman, and his face was in deep shadow under the peak of his kepi. He stooped and picked up the box; handed it to her.

"Nothing breakable in here, I hope." He was quite young, and he seemed to be smiling. When she didn't reply, he added: "You would do better to keep to the lighted paths. Are you a tourist?"

"Yes."

"American?"

"English."

Glancing, she saw that the youths were sauntering back to their seat, laughing and unconcerned.

"Good night, mam'selle." He saluted. "I hope you have a pleasant stay in Paris."

"Thank you."

She went on. There was nothing ahead but the floodlit façade of the Petit Palais. She was running out of darkness and concealment. In a few moments, she would be among the noise and the lights and the people again.

The glare of the floodlights blinded her to the way ahead. She felt rain-softened earth yield beneath her shoes, and, looking down, saw that she was walking across a circular patch set with spring flowers. In an instant of great release, she saw what she must do.

She scrabbled with her hands and dug a hole among the tulips. It was too dark to see, but she heard the thing flop out of the shoebox and into its shallow grave. The earth was soon scooped back. She crushed up the box; a few minutes later she dropped it into a waste-paper basket in the Champs Élysées; and now it seemed that no one in all the self-absorbed stream of strollers cared enough to glance at her.

The walk back to the hotel was like the slow awakening from a nightmare; she was even sufficiently conscious of her normal functions as to crave for a cooling drink.

There was a black Citroën parked on the same side as, and close by, the hotel. As she neared it, the headlights pulsed a sudden signal, and a man put his head out of the rear window.

"Good evening, Miss Jeans. Been enjoying a little stroll?" said Superintendent Haquin.

Haquin offered her a cigarette, which she refused. The rosy glow of his lighter did nothing to soften his heavy, peasant features: deeply lined wrinkles stretched from the nostrils to below the full-lipped mouth; the lumpish end of the nose was like an afterthought; feathery gray eyebrows shielded from her his downcast glance.

She felt hemmed in and imprisoned. Outside the car, the uncaring world walked by, and neon lights flashed on and off. The world of people and things had no regard for the private agony of Candida Jeans.

"You interest me, Miss Jeans, do you know that?"

"Do I?" She put her hands out of sight and clenched them tightly. He's playing with me, she thought. This is the beginning of cat-and-mouse. He *knows*. . . .

"Yes, you interest me very much. There is a quality about you that I have met with only rarely in young ladies like yourself—not that it has been my fortune to meet many young ladies like yourself." He smiled. "Now, I can see that I am embarrassing you. Am I embarrassing the lady—do you sense that, Martin?"

"A little, perhaps, sir." The flaxen-haired young man in

the front seat spoke in heavily accented English, without turning round.

Candida glanced at him, and saw that his rear-view mirror was adjusted so as to watch her. When their eyes met, he reached up and slid the mirror to one side.

There was a pause of silence; then Haquin spoke in a flat, matter-of-fact voice. She saw that he had taken out a notebook.

"You will be interested to hear the latest developments in the regrettable matter that so upset you yesterday. By the way, I hope that you are feeling much better. . . ."

"Yes. The—shock—has worn off now."

"The human mind is very resilient," said Haquin, "and hard work is a great help. As I was saying, there are developments. The London police have been making inquiries, and are still continuing. You and your companions were quite correct in your assumptions about the students you encountered in the airport bar: they were, in fact, medical students. They were bound for a tour of Rugby football matches in Belgium. So much for that."

A thin sensation of hope caused Candida to relax her tensed fingers.

"They were contacted this morning, in Liège. All stoutly denied that they were drunk and noisy—which is immaterial —or that they played the trick of putting a severed hand in anyone's luggage. . . ."

The two-noted call of a fire engine rose to drown Haquin to silence. The vehicle swept past, lights winking in time to the blare, and turned down past the Madeleine. The traffic started moving again.

"Regrettably," resumed Haquin, "our pathologist's report also rules out the medical student angle. I won't go into upsetting and gruesome details, Miss Jeans, but the thing that turned up in your luggage was not in the particular condition of anatomical specimens available in medical schools, you understand."

She felt that he was waiting for her to say something, but her mouth was too dry to get round words that weren't there anyhow.

"Well, that's all, Miss Jeans."

She glanced at him in surprise. He was smiling at her.

"I just thought you'd like to know how things were going," he said. "It's been very pleasant talking to you."

Then the flaxen-haired driver was opening the passenger door for her to get out. He, too, was smiling.

"We'll meet again," said Inspector Haquin, taking her hand, "and when we do, perhaps you'll be sufficiently intrigued as to ask me what it is about you that I find so interesting— and perhaps I shall be able to overcome my natural diffidence and talk to you about it. Good night, Miss Jeans."

The flaxen-haired man opened the hotel door for her. She went straight to the reception desk, where the clerk was bowed over a newspaper. No, there was no mail for room number forty-six.

Candida went up alone in the crawling little lift, with voices crowding in on her; she pressed her cheek against the mirrored wall and closed her eyes, willing one of the speaking faces to come alive in her mind.

Jeremy, if only you could have written a few lines. Just a few lines, to see me through tonight, and tomorrow, and the next day. . . .

Brighton, she and Jeremy Stanton had decided, was ludicrously ooh-la-la; surely the fat shade of Prince Regent flitted, every night, from his pretty wedding cake of a Pavilion, to gaze approvingly at the goings-on in his favorite resort.

They had driven down for the races. Candida—who
had never been to a race meeting before—enjoyed the spec-
tacle and the horses, but was put out by the amount of
money that Jeremy quite cheerfully lost. Afterward, they
sat and had drinks in the palm court of a big hotel on the
promenade; speculating about the other couples—most of
whom showed great disparity in ages, to the advantage of
the women. Jeremy tagged them variously as bosses and
their secretaries, or showgirls and their agents.

Candida was beginning to get used to this kind of talk. It
fitted in, she told herself, with his frank innocence; his knack
of making light of subjects that Mummy would have dis-
missed as unmentionable. At the level of the relationship
that had developed between them—they had been out together three times—it was completely acceptable, even re-
freshing. She told herself that she was growing up at last;
popping her nose out of the nest, and not disliking the
smell of the big world beyond.

It had been quite easy and acceptable, in this context, to
fall in with his sudden idea of staying overnight in Brighton,
so that they could enjoy a late, leisurely dinner. Of course,
she had no luggage and neither had he, but—model-like—she
carried half a beautician's shop in her oversized handbag,
including a toothbrush. Would they be able to get rooms on
a race day? Jeremy thought so, and came back later to say
it was fixed.

Over dinner, they elaborated on the imaginary backgrounds
of the people around them. A four-piece ensemble playing
gems from musical shows was hilarious. Their elderly waitress
took a shine to Jeremy, and he responded with a lot of
boyish play with his forelock and alluring eyelash flickering,
so that Candida nearly choked into her napkin.

She was light-headed with wine and laughter when they

went upstairs together. They held hands, and she privately decided that the time had come to surprise him with a good-night kiss on the lips when they parted at her door.

The euphoria died when he followed her into what she had supposed was her own room, closing and locking the door behind him.

She got her first terror under control, and tried to reason with him. It was obvious that he was indulgently amused, but the playfulness with which he removed the door key and put it in his pocket was soon replaced by exasperation. Did she, for Christ's sake, expect him to believe that she was still a wilting virgin after—how long was it—five years in the modeling game?

She tried patience then: without offering any explanations, she simply asked him to unlock the door and let her go. His reaction was to take off his shirt and start washing his teeth.

The violence, when it came, was all from her side. Later, nearly naked, he leaped out of the bed and approached where she was sitting, stiffly upright and quaking, her handbag on her knees. He was smilingly persuasive as he came toward her. Surely she wasn't going to stay up all night in the cold?

Even when she took out nail scissors, he remained good-humored; advancing his hand toward her shrinking shoulder and telling her not to be a silly puss.

Then she struck. Blindly.

"You murderous little bitch! God, you'd kill a man to hang on to it, wouldn't you?"

There was nothing she could find to say as she watched him wash the slash on his forearm and bind it up with his handkerchief, then throw himself sulkily into bed and snap off the light.

In the dark, sleepless hours, Candida sat listening to the

traffic on the lighted promenade outside the window, and to his heavy breathing; all the while keeping up a silent dialogue with him; explaining how it was impossible for her, because she was different from everyone else—a dead and cauterized personality inside the shell of a woman; that she was sorry, because she would have wished to have made him happy, in return for filling an emptiness in her life.

She was still awake—and the words had not been spoken aloud—when morning came, and they went down to a silent breakfast. He drove back to London unnecessarily fast, and dropped her outside her flat without saying good-bye.

A week later, he telephoned her with an invitation to lunch. When they met, he treated her as if Brighton had never been—and by then she was quite sure that she was in love with Jeremy Stanton.

◄ FIVE ►

ALL PARIS was gray again in the morning, under a steady downpour of rain that showed no promise of letting up.

Unaccountably, Sonia Hammersley was tautly amusing in the taxi. She even addressed a few sprightly remarks to Candida; but switched her attention to Lubbock when nothing bounced back. He was as responsive as ever.

Candida stared out of the streaming windows, blind to midmorning workaday Paris. Two capsules had given her a few hours of sleep that had been haunted by nightmares which were disastrously easy to recall: ballets of wavering hands and a sensation that Jeremy Stanton was screaming at her from the remote end of an echoing corridor.

They went into the cemetery of Père Lachaise by a side entrance: an archway at the end of the high wall fronting the Avenue Gambetta, up a flight of rain-streaming steps. Ahead of them, a complex of graveled paths snaked up the slopes of the enclosed City of the Dead, lined with dwarf temples in the classical style, specimens of lesser Chartres, a grotesquely attenuated Rheims.

There was nobody in sight. "Good thing, too," said Sonia Hammersley. "I knew we'd never get official permission to shoot fashion pictures in here, so I never tried—which is why we didn't traipse in through the front gates with egg on our faces and all our bag and baggage."

She unfolded a map of the cemetery, shielding it from the downpour with her umbrella. "It marks all the really interesting graves and mausoleums here," she said. "I checked it through again last night, and I decided we should start by shooting the chiffon thing beside Chopin's grave—the romantic theme—and the black-and-white *art nouveau* print against Oscar Wilde's, that'll be a nice allusive touch. Sarah Bernhardt's somewhere, as well as Héloïs and Abélard."

Candida stared helplessly down at the black mackintosh and boots she was wearing.

"You'll change wherever the hell we can find a spot of shelter, darling," purred Sonia, "even if it has to be under an umbrella. Hilary, your job will be to get your pictures before the rain's plastered the lines of the garments into nonsense."

Hilary Lubbock was elated: all excited creativity that shut him off from any awareness of the two girls' taut attitudes.

"I was dead wrong about the stonemasons' yard yesterday afternoon," he said. "This is going to be the high spot of the sequence. What a joint! You'll scrap all the other prints when you see what we turn out today. This is the Black Look. Drenched. That's how I see it now—drenched in somber, poetic romance. Dripping stonework. Cypresses shivering in the rain. Ruination and wet lichen. Forgotten glories . . ."

He was already crouched—dark hair splayed in fronds across his wet brow, and Hasselblad clacking—before the façade of a squat Doric temple, whose streaked iron doors was hung with a worn marble chaplet.

"Never mind about the slim quarto volume of arty pictures that's going to win you immortality, love," said Sonia Hammersley, "Let's get *this* bloody show on the road."

She led the way up a curved path signposted Avenue Fred. Seulie. Hilary Lubbock followed, shoulders hunched under the weight of the suitcase and camera gear. Candida came after them. Three wet stragglers in the City of the Dead. Past the lines of silent, regarding mausoleums; toward the heart of the cemetery that rose, pinnacle above pinnacle and roof above roof, to the steeple of a distant chapel that poked above the hillcrest beyond a stand of blossoming chestnut trees. As they climbed higher, they could hear the dull boom of the traffic in the Avenue Gambetta below them.

They passed no one but a man and a pale-faced boy walking hand-in-hand. The child carried a sheaf of daffodils, and the man was whistling through his teeth; both of them stared stonily ahead.

The avenue ended in a roundabout with a domed, classical monument in the center: a circular amphitheater walled by dripping tombs, with four paths leading off round secret corners.

"I'm lost," said Sonia Hammersley. "This place is nothing but a goddamned maze!" She unfolded the plan, but it had turned into a limp, wet rag. "I had Chopin pinpointed just now. He's marked 17E somewhere on this thing."

"Give us a squint," said Lubbock. "What a mess!"

They were saved by the arrival of a couple of policemen, patrolling the rain-drenched maze of mausoleums against heaven knows what obscure crimes. Candida turned her back, hiding her face from them, while they gave cheerful directions: straight up the Avenue des Wilantes, they said; turn left up the Avenue Neigre and cross in front of the chapel to the Chemin Denon; and the tomb of M. Chopin was a couple of hundred meters on the left, set back from the path.

It was a simple, low wall with a headstone that barely rose above the rank grass surrounding it.

Frédéric Chopin
17 Octobre 1849

Candida posed beside the headstone, waiting till Hilary Lubbock had decided where to stand, and was crouched with his eye to the viewfinder, before she shrugged out of the wet mack and shook out the flimsy folds of chiffon skirt which were gathered up round her waist. Last of all, she threw aside her rain hat.

"Do a sort of Isadora Duncan thing," said Lubbock. "Raise your arms up and look up at the sky. Lovely. Lovely. Now the mourning vestal-virgin bit—make it broad and theatrical. Great."

"Fluff out the skirt before it gets soaked," said Sonia Hammersley. "Oh, gawd, it's lost all its bounce already. Cut, Hilary!"

Candid's skin suddenly prickled to see a white-faced woman watching her from the narrow space between two mausoleums down by the path. She was bare-headed, wore a coarse apron, and carried—astonishingly—a dustpan and broom. She was waiting for them when they reached the path again; standing by the partly open door of a mausoleum that revealed a dusty interior like a small chapel, with an altar. There was a straw shopping bag set upon the altar, between sheaves of dead flowers.

The woman ignored the others. She held out her hand toward Candida, palm upmost, and animal sounds came out of her straining throat. She was probably quite young, but some infirmity had arched and twisted her back, and her ashen skin gave a preternatural appearance. Candida shrank away before the stare of the vacant eyes and the toothless mouthings, as if from a leper.

"Trust *you* to fascinate a nut case!" snapped Sonia. "For heaven's sake, give her some money, Hilary, and let's get on. No—wait!" She pushed open the door of the tiny mausoleum to its full limit and looked inside.

The stone floor was slimy with ancient greenness and the crazed plaster walls were hung with dark swags of grimy cobwebs in all the corners. The eye of faith could just pick out where someone—presumably the imbecile cleaning woman —had cleared a small patch on the floor with a stiff broom. Above the small altar, an oval-topped window thinly let in the daylight through dirty rectangles of blue-and-red glass.

"It's not a model's dressing room at Grave Vale," said Sonia, "but it does mean we don't have to ruin the black-and-white *art nouveau* by trying to squeeze her into it under an umbrella."

Candida edged back from the door. "Sonia—I couldn't un-dress in *there!*"

"Don't be so damn' ridiculous! While Hilary's shooting under these ghastly conditions, you'll have to sink your stupid, mimsy scruples and cooperate. You'll change into the black-and-white here, where it's dry, and then we'll go and look for Oscar Wilde."

She turned to the cleaning woman, who was standing un-concernedly in the downpour, with rat tails of wispy hair hung round her thin cheeks.

"Will it be all right if my friend uses this place as a

changing-room for a few minutes?" And when the woman
continued to stare vacantly at Candida: "Oh, God! Hilary,
give her something quite substantial—a ten-franc note or
something—and try a bit of miming."

In the end, their intention seemed to get through to the
cleaning woman, and she fussed to help Lubbock carry the
suitcase and lay it on the cleaner spot of the floor. She
nodded and pointed to Candida when Sonia Hammersley
shook out the black-and-white print dress.

"We'll leave you to it," said Sonia. "Don't be long."

"You're not going far away?" said Candida, suddenly
alarmed.

"We're going to find what shelter we can under the nearest
tree," said the other. "Oh, for heaven's sake, girl! We can't
all crowd in here. It's not much bigger than a blessed loo."

"Call us when you're ready, Candy," said Lubbock. He
winked at her, and closed the door. She saw his silhouette
briefly framed in the panel of dingy green glass that was
striped with a pattern of rusty wrought iron and set in the
upper part of the door. Above the drumming of the rain on
the roof above her head, she heard their footsteps fading
away up the path outside. Then she was alone.

In her haste to change quickly and get out of the sinister
little cell, she forgot to unfasten the neck of the dress, and
a full minute of claustrophobic struggling inside the wet material drained the last of her self-control. She shrank when
her bare skin came in contact with the dank air; hugged herself and looked down at the flesh that was suddenly unfamiliar
in the cold light from the colored glass of the window.

Into the black-and-white print, a quick repair to her make-
up, and get out . . .

She stepped into the dress and zipped it up.

Make-up . . .

Then she remembered. All her bits and pieces were in an airline bag that Sonia Hammersley had lent her—and Sonia was still carrying it, slung over her shoulder.

Turning, she reached out for the latch of the door—and saw a face flattened against the green glass; a rubbery nose and mouth screwed into a monstrous grimace.

She screamed when the latch clacked upward. She was still screaming, and fighting against the thing that was trying to get through the door, when Lubbock and Sonia Hammersley came running. She yielded the door to Lubbock and sagged back against the wall with her eyes closed.

"Easy on, duckie. No one's going to hurt you." Lubbock's hand was on her shoulder.

"For crying out loud. Does she want us to get slung out of the damn' cemetery neck and crop?" asked Sonia Hammersley.

Candida opened her eyes, and the idiot cleaning woman was staring at her in slack-lipped dismay. She had the airline bag in her hands; turning it over and over.

"It really wasn't very bright of you to send her with the bag," said Lubbock.

"Why not?" demanded Sonia Hammersley. "Why should I traipse round after that hysterical little cow?" But there was no anger in her face; that was only a veneer of pretense. What Candida saw there—and the unexpectedness of it registered with surprising clarity in her shocked mind—was gloating amusement. As if Sonia had staged the whole thing with premeditation and malice.

A slight check in the downpour made the first quarter-hour of the search for Oscar Wilde's tomb not too physically unpleasant. Hilary Lubbock, with his ability to shrug off an atmosphere of tension, responded with schoolboyish delight to the illustrious—or sometimes absurdly bombastic—names that appeared, all unexpectedly, on the time-worn monoliths which cluttered the borders of the maze. A scaled-down Gothic cathedral inscribed with generations of a ducal family, whose sonorous roll-call of ministers, cardinals, generals, and presidents of this and that appeared to have been snuffed out into oblivion around the turn of the century, carried overtones of pathetic banality. But, said Lubbock, here was a name to juggle with; a piece of the tremendous past trumpeting into a wet Wednesday morning.

There was a youngish French couple standing before the black marble tomb. They looked like tourists up from the provinces, determined to squeeze the last drop of experience out of Paris, rain or no rain. They buttonholed Candida because she happened to be nearest. Was this indeed the well-known marshal? they asked her; and she—shaken out of her numbed withdrawal from things about her—had to appeal to Lubbock. He was able to assure the couple, in his flamboyantly inaccurate French, that the black marble indeed shrouded the bones of Michel Ney, Bravest of the Brave, shot by a firing squad after Waterloo, but—he was pleased to add with a smug grin—by your lot, not our lot. They didn't understand, but thanked Lubbock. The encounter seemed to raise his spirits a few notches higher.

After that, the downpour started again.

They were toiling up a curved avenue that seemed like a hundred others they had trodden before. The rain had given up any pretense, and the whole world was a wall of solid water. Huddled beneath her umbrella, Candida was breathing fine spray, even inside her high plastic collar. Her legs were soaked to the thighs. Under the streaming mackintosh, a cold trickle told her that even the black-and-white dress was not escaping the searching wetness.

Now she was walking in a limbo that could never end, with her pounded nerves quiescent at last. Her recollection of the moments of horror in the little mausoleum were on the same plane of unreality as the tall tombs, the great trees, and the roaring waste of water.

Lubbock was plunging along ahead of her. He had no umbrella. Having taken off his windcheater to drape over the camera gear that hung from his shoulder, he was soaked to the skin.

He shouted to Sonia Hammersley, who was leading.

"Let's call it a day and come back tomorrow. Hell, Sonia, even if we find Oscar Wilde, I can't get pictures in these conditions, and Candy will be drenched as soon as she takes off the mack."

No reply. Sonia didn't even turn round.

They rounded another corner, and the avenue rose steeply beyond it, hemmed in on each side by more soaring marble and granite.

"Sonia, we've been this way before!" shouted Lubbock.

"No, we haven't. It all *looks* the same, that's all."

"There's Ney's tomb again. We passed it—heaven knows, it seems like a million years ago." He turned and appealed to Candida. Arms spread wide, he looked like a body dragged from the sea. "You remember, don't you, Candy?"

"What's the use in asking her?" snapped Sonia Hammersley. "All right, then. So we've come round in a circle, but the section we're looking for is somewhere up ahead. It's just a matter of not taking the wrong turning again."

They went on, cresting a rise, to a plateau. And now the avenues were laid out in a grid of straight lines, and they could see the boundary wall in the distance and the irregular rooftops of the houses beyond it. The rain began to slacken.

"The avenue we want is somewhere along here," said Sonia,

pointing. "One of those leading down to the wall. It may be the next one, or the one after."

"You can try the first one," said Lubbock firmly. "If you draw a blank, come back to this spot. Candy and I'll look down the next one."

Sonia Hammersley went off without a word, and Lubbock cupped his hand under Candida's elbow. "Come on, ducks. Even a few minutes away from our little Sonia's going to be a relief for all concerned."

Hilary Lubbock spotted it quite easily. They crossed another transverse avenue, and the tomb was on their left: a squared-off block enclosing a naked, winged figure.

"Oscar Fingal O'Flahertie Wills Wilde," said Lubbock, running his palm over the wet stonework. "Funny, but even in this permissive age, I can't think of him as a persecuted martyr. He didn't have a martyr's style. Indolence, cynicism, and good talk was Oscar's style, and it became him very well; he probably did that better than anyone who's ever lived. But he could sometimes write like an angel, and he had real humanity."

There were a few half-dead flowers lying on a ledge: most of them were single carnations.

"We should have brought a green carnation," said Lubbock. "He'd have liked that, poor Oscar."

The words came to Candida through a wall of numb self-absorption. She was tracing the smooth line of the carved wing with her finger when Lubbock slid his arm round her waist, and she stiffened with a sudden sense of peril.

"Candy, isn't there anything I can do to help you?"

She closed her eyes and made a half-turn to disengage his hand. And he kissed her full on the lips.

"You grubby, underhand creeps!"

It was Sonia Hammersley, watching them from the other side of the avenue. She must have cut across, between the tombs, and the grass had muffled her footsteps. Candida broke free and leaned back against Wilde's tomb.

"Oh, come off it, Sonia," growled Lubbock.

"I suppose you had a quiet little natter together and set up this sordid little tête-à-tête," shrilled Sonia Hammersley. Her pale eyes were on Candida; Lubbock might not have existed. "You mimsy, necrophilic little whore!"

"Candy!" shouted Lubbock.

But she was running; ducking round the close-set monuments. He was coming after her. She could hear his footfalls swishing through the rank grass, and getting closer.

"Candy—wait!"

He cornered her in front of a slab of lichened granite that blocked her path. She edged away from the touch of his hands at her waist; pressed her face against the cold stone and willed everything around her to become someone else's experience. As a child, she had had the ability to do this: to say to herself that she was not there; but that someone else was looking out, through her eyes, onto a scene suddenly turned dreamlike and unsubstantial. She tried it now, but the stone was hard and wet—and his hands had a reality that made her soul shrink.

"Please," he pleaded. "I'm sorry, Candy. Truly, I wasn't —I hadn't planned to get you alone to make a pass at you. And that was a lousy thing that Sonia said. Better forget it."

He slid one hand from her waist to her shoulder, trying to turn her.

"Look at me."

She faced him then, and what he saw made him lower his hands.

"If you touch me again, Hilary," she said flatly, "I think I shall go mad."

She looked down as he backed away from her, but she could guess his expression. He stood irresolutely for a few moments—then turned to go back to where he had left Sonia Hammersley.

"I'm soiled," she said aloud. "I'll never be clean in all my life, no matter what I do. And I destroy everyone who tries to get near me."

She had learned to ingratiate herself, and had found it to be the only way of winning affection. . . .

What she overheard that Sunday night of the television episode gave shape and meaning to some of Mummy's attitudes which had formerly puzzled and upset her: the withdrawing from impulsive embraces; the way she always kissed good night on the forehead; her dislike of holding hands when they were out walking together. It occurred to the sensitive eleven-year-old child that her mother lumped her together with dirty-pawed cats, pictures that were hung awry, dog mess on pavements, and the people in the council estate across the road—and it had something to do with her dead father, of whom she had no remembrance.

Her father had done something wrong, something dirty; which was why his name was so seldom mentioned, and why there was only a solitary photograph of him in the house, and that a snapshot taken with his parents on Skegness pier when he was a boy.

Her father being only a name and an unformed face in a faded snapshot, it seemed to Candida that by trying very hard she must be able to shake off what had to be a very tenuous influence. She was soiled. Well, then, she would clean herself. Then Mummy would love her without reservations—as she loved Wissie when he was curled up asleep on a cushion with his paws well wiped.

It was a long walk into the sunlight, and it cost hard work, patience and sacrifice. Only gradually did Mummy begin to notice—and approve—the change in Candida.

In practical, humdrum matters, the child took on more chores around the house. There was tea in bed for Mummy every morning, and even she was not able to fault the cleanliness of the china, though she checked on it. While Mummy was cooking breakfast, the whine of the vacuum cleaner was to be heard somewhere in the house; and Candida always found a job to do in the kitchen before she started her evening's homework.

A withdrawn child, she had only two friends: girls in her form at school who lived nearby. They had been in the habit of playing in each other's gardens on Saturday afternoons, but this stopped—and Mummy was pleased, because the Jones girl and the Summers girl had rather common accents.

In the delicate area of their personal relationship, Candida showed an instinctive subtlety; spending more time in Mummy's company, yet at the same time keeping a tactile distance. No more impulsive hugging. No attempt to sneak a good-night kiss on the lips when only a forehead was offered.

The breakthrough came in the summer of her thirteenth year, when she won an open scholarship to the local girls' day public school; when Mummy bought a bottle of cream sherry for a Sunday-morning celebration. After a glass and a half, Mummy let down her hair and told Uncle Bernard that Candida was a daughter of whom any mother would be proud.

She had wandered into a walled court: a Wall of the Dead, with names and dates inscribed on small rectangles of stone and brass, six tiers high. In the middle of the court was a squat black temple in the Egyptian style, with bulging columns and lotus-head capitals. It had chimneys.

There was a group of people coming toward her: pale Scandinavians in fawn raincoats, and some of them were laughing together. She drew back against the wall, and looked away till they had gone past. A boy who was loitering in the rear saw her and came toward her. He was smiling: washed-out blue eyes behind rimless glasses.

"What time is the conducted tour of the crematorium, please?" he asked, in badly accented French.

She ran.

Home and refuge were the hotel, and somehow she had to get there. The end of a long avenue brought her, blessedly, to the same steps by which they had entered Père Lachaise.

She stood by the curb, watching the traffic swooping past on the broad avenue. It had begun to drizzle with rain, and all the taxis were taken. Walking was out of the question; the thought of losing herself in the alien streets, and having to appeal for help, was intolerable.

She saw the Metro station entrance on the opposite corner—Martin-Nadaud—and ran toward it. At the bottom of the steps, the swing doors let through a gust of overheated air that stirred the wet skirt under her mackintosh. She bowed her head and walked to join a queue alongside the booking office.

"Yes?"

She looked up, to see a sharp-featured woman glaring at her aggressively through the glass screen.

"A ticket, please."

"First or second class?"

"It—doesn't matter. Second. Give me second, please."

"Two francs."

Candida fumbled in the pockets of her mackintosh, and knew that she would find nothing there. Someone sniggered in the queue behind her. Taking out her hands, she looked down at her left wrist, and had an impulse to tear off her watch and give it to the woman in return for the precious fragment of pasteboard that was her passport to the sanctuary of her hotel room.

"Mam'selle! You are holding up all these people."

"Please . . ."

"Please *what*, mam'selle?" The woman looked affronted.

A man's hand came into her line of vision, on the worn brass strip beneath the window. It slid a coin under the glass.

"I have the young lady's fare."

She looked round—into the smiling, avuncular face of Superintendent Haquin.

They were strap-hanging together in the swaying carriage, and there was no escaping his searching regard. A youth in a blue workman's jacket was sitting right by her hip, his hand firmly clamped in the hand of a girl who was glaring up at Candida through a valance of long blonde hair. No escape for her eyes in that direction.

Between Martin-Nadaud and Montmartre, Haquin said nothing; he had said nothing when he had limped beside her down to the platform. But he was watching her all the time. And her skin crawled.

The train stopped, and she swayed against him. He steadied her.

"You're wet through."

She nodded.

The doors slid open with a hiss of escaping air, and a lot of people left the carriage. Haquin guided her to the seats where the boy and girl had been sitting. She sat down and saw her reflection darkly mirrored in the opposite window: white-faced, with drawn-in cheeks and shadowed cavities for eyes.

"Where are your colleagues?" asked Haquin pleasantly. "Surely you've not been wandering alone in the rain." And when she didn't reply: "Well, then, it was a happy chance that we met. Think of it: in all Paris, I should come across the very young lady who interests me so much, and be able to perform a small service for her."

A little later, he said: "We change at the next stop." Do I tell him? she thought. He's waiting for me to tell him, playing with me; but soon the smiling will have to stop, and all the following me around. He knows—or guesses—why I went out last evening, but he'd rather I told him myself. Soon he'll grow tired of waiting and watching, then he'll accuse me. So why not tell him now, before the train stops? Shake off this hideous thing and let him make what he likes of it. Count up to five, and then blurt it out: I, Candida Jeans, am haunted by pieces of dead flesh and bone that concern me very nearly, because—on account of the way I am and the way I have been in the past—I know that they must have some connection with the destructiveness that's inside me.

The train slowed to a halt. The opportunity passed, and her half-formed resolution with it.

They changed to another line, and it was only one station to the Madeleine. Haquin walked with her to the hotel. He gave a ducking little bow as he opened the door for her.

"Good-bye again, Miss Jeans. We really must have that illuminating conversation some time."

There was a familiar figure behind the reception desk: a stocky man in his middle fifties, with the wavy hair and Ronald Coleman moustache of a latter-day Riviera gigolo.

"Miss Jeans! How nice. I missed your late arrival on Monday because I went off duty."

"Hello, Charles."

She had known—and liked—Charles ever since her first stay at the hotel. Nothing was too much trouble for him, and his air of time-worn gallantry was easy to take. Now he was winking at her in the buttonholing Gallic manner that carries the overtones of sex without tears.

"You received the letter all right Miss Jeans?"

"Letter?" She stared at him uncomprehendingly.

The clerk clicked his tongue in mild annoyance; moistened a finger and trailed it along one gray-flecked eyebrow.

"Tch! Miss Hammersley said most particularly that she'd remember to hand it to you as soon as you arrived. Never mind. She came in with Mr. Lubbock half an hour ago. You'll find her in her room."

◀ SIX ▶

ONCE IN HER own room, Candida's sudden delight was marginally flattened by the practicalities of asking Sonia Hammersley for the letter. Sonia had stupidly forgotten to give it to her on Monday, of course; but her own hideously embarrassing behavior in Père Lachaise—for, with the joy and deliverance of a letter from Jeremy after all, her recent nightmarish state of mind had completely dissipated, leaving her with the wry conviction that the whole thing had been her own fault and that she had made a hysterical fool of herself—hardly left her in a position to carp over a piece of thoughtlessness. No snappy rebuke to Sonia, certainly; but how to face her, after what had happened in the cemetery?

She toyed with the idea of ringing through to the room along the corridor and casually asking the other to slip the letter under her door, because she was undressed and just about to pop into a bath; but it sounded contrived, and she rejected it.

Nothing to do but go round to Room 44, ask for the letter and take whatever punishment Sonia's sharp tongue handed out. There would be the letter to hang onto: a reassuring talisman against the other's contempt—and against everything else.

First the black-and-white dress. No point in giving Sonia yet another lever against her: the dress was on loan from the manufacturers to the magazine. Take it off and hang it up.

This she did; put on her dressing gown and smoothed down her damp hair. A few moments later, she was tapping on the door of Room 44.

No reply. She heard the sound of running bath water.

She tried the handle. The door was unlocked and it swung open to her touch. The bedroom was empty of everything but the tatterdemalion mess of an essentially untidy female: underwear and a pair of discarded tights lay in the middle of the floor; a jumble of clothes half hung out of an open suitcase; the bedclothes were awry, so presumably Sonia had been resting before her bath; a half-smoked cigarette still burned in an ashtray on the bedside table—and something lay beside the ashtray: an envelope.

"Anyone there?"

It came from the bathroom, above the sound of the running water. It should have been answered, and Candida would have answered it—but she was already crossing the room, and her hand was reaching out toward the white rectangle on the bedside table.

The Grave Vale imprint—a leopard rampant enclosed in a cartouche—was embossed in black on the torn flap, and it was this that had attracted her eyes from across the room. Wonderingly, she turned the thing over: it was addressed to her at the hotel.

Her fingers trembled when they took out the single sheet of office writing paper. The message was typed—badly typed, with mis-struck letters brutally hammered over, handwritten corrections, and a spilt stain defacing one corner—in the way that only Jeremy Stanton knew how. And his elegant Italic scrawl leaped out at her from the superscription:

Candyfloss. Eternal jade. Burner of the
topless towers of Illium . . .

Beyond the bathroom door came the sound of water gurgling away, and the thump of a bare limb hitting the side of the bath. Sonia Hammersley was coming out. Candida had a wayward impulse to be standing where she was, with the violated letter in her hand, to meet the other's shocked glance when the door opened; instead, she walked swiftly out of the bedroom and shut the door behind her.

She took the letter, but left the envelope where it was.

Being peaky was definitely in, some of them told her; the hollow-eyed and haunted thing went with the trendy flavor of *art nouveau* and the skinny line of the current shroud look—but wasn't darling Candida overdoing it, perhaps? A motherly studio stylist had taken her aside and asked her if she was pregnant; when she had a persistent cough during most of the winter, someone suggested she should have her chest X-rayed for possible tuberculosis of the lungs.

They were all quite wrong; she was neither physically ailing nor *enceinte;* and in the months of her association with Jeremy Stanton she gazed sadly from the covers of some of the very best magazines, on the strength of which her agent managed to negotiate a considerable increase in her modeling fees.

No one knew, or suspected anything, about her and Stanton. Candida, almost uniquely for a top model, had never been part of the magazine and fashion world's social merry-go-round—the party at which they had met had been her first and last—so no one knew of the change in her personal life. She was too arcane to give her confidences to the dressing-room set.

Their affair added up to about two meetings a week and some telephone calls. He always picked her up at her mews flat, tooting the car horn as a signal of his arrival. He never set foot in the flat; since the disastrous night in Brighton, they had never been alone in a room together. In the evenings, they drove to some suburban pub or restaurant, where Stanton drank his minimal six whiskies, then talked till closing time, while Candida watched and listened. A weekend afternoon meeting meant a walk in the park, a visit to the zoo, or maybe a film show. He detested the theater because, he said, he lacked the capacity for a willing suspension of disbelief. They sometimes held hands, but never kissed.

A mild winter faded almost unnoticed into spring, and Candida wished—though it was tearing her apart—that their relationship could go on forever. What he had to offer her was enough for her needs, which were related to the happiest memories of her life with Mummy, when they had sat opposite each other in the cosy living room at St. Aubyn, and just chatted about this and that. What she gave in return, she was aware, was practically nothing; not quite true—she was an admiring audience, who marveled at the effortless precision with which he expressed ideas, without the self-conscious "ums" and "you-knows" and "sort-ofs" that sprinkled the speech of most people she knew. She also tried to make herself look attractive for him; was conscious that he admired her looks, and took a pride in her when they were in public together.

She supposed that he still wanted her—was perhaps, indeed, biding his time for another opportunity of seduction—but he never showed any signs of it; no seemingly accidental touching, though he sometimes slipped his hand round her waist to guide her through a crowded restaurant.

The debilitating fear she lived with, her sleeping and waking dread, was that Stanton would grow tired of her and chuck her. And why not? He was a normal, red-blooded man with a man's needs; working in a business that was full of normal, obliging, and attractive girls only too ready to match his needs.

Sometimes, desperation took over. During the winter, when a bad cold had left her with a dry cough and no appetite, when her empty evenings were spent writing him letters that were never posted, she kidded herself—knowing all the time that it was beyond her—that she would call him from the window, in a chiffon nightdress, when next he came to collect her.

He never spoke of his personal life outside their relationship. The likelihood that he might be sleeping with other girls scarcely troubled her, and she rationalized this by supposing that there could hardly be jealousy without desire.

Stanton was concerned in the April trip to Paris because the Black Look feature was being shot for his paper. They arranged to meet for a farewell dinner on the Saturday evening, but he rang her late on Friday night and told her it was off: Monday was press day, and he was so far behind with the work that he was having to take home a pile of stuff which would keep him hard at it all over the weekend.

Candida pleaded: couldn't she come round to his flat and spend Saturday with him? She'd be as quiet as a mouse and not get in his hair. She could cook his meals and tackle any chores that needed to be done around the place.

Stanton thought for a while, then said it wouldn't work—but that he'd meet her for a couple of hours in the afternoon.

They went to the zoo. Stanton, who had had nothing to drink, was distinctly below par. Even the primates—who could usually be relied on to provoke him to be his best and wittiest—fell flat. When it rained, they sat in the crowded restaurant and drank a lot of tea, while Stanton looked at his watch too often, and Candida knew—with a clear and jewel-like certainty—that this was going to be their last time together, because she would come back from Paris to find that he had chucked her.

When they parted, it was she who impulsively kissed him, and made him promise to write to her, straight away, so that the letter would be waiting for her when she arrived in Paris. Then she watched him drive away—and out of her life.

That evening, she cleaned the flat from top to bottom, and packed up a lot of rubbish to be thrown away. The television held her attention for about five minutes. After that, she cooked herself quite an elaborate supper—but decided she was not hungry, and put it down for the cat.

The cat was missing.

He was an elderly tabby with a standoffish manner which she had inherited along with the furniture and fittings of the flat. He seldom strayed and was fed by the caretaker when she was away for any length of time. She told herself she was worried for him: after that it only took about half an hour of walking up and down to convince herself that she should ring up Jeremy Stanton and ask him to come round to help in the search.

She heard the number ring out, but there was no answer.

After a long time, she replaced the receiver and focused her gaze on the print of a Corot landscape above the telephone table.

He wasn't at home. No pile of weekend work for Jeremy. He'd lied to her; he was out. And not alone. He was with another girl—one who was able to give herself. . . .

There was a paper knife lying by the telephone. She saw her hand reach out and take it up; raise it on high, like a dagger, and drive it deeply into the table top. She was still staring in disbelief at what she had done, when the tabby sidled up and gave her ankle a tentative rub with his ear.

Candyfloss. Eternal jade. Burner of the topless towers of Illium,

It is very, very late on Saturday night. Correction—it is very, very early on Sunday morning; but the last thing I shall do before I creep into my virginal bed will be to go out and post this at the corner.

Department of confessions. Tonight I have exceeded—lavishly exceeded—the required six Scotches that raise me to par, and I have gone far beyond euphoria. I am, in fact, just about as drunk as a man can be and still get some kind of coherence out of this infernal typing machine.

You asked me to write you in Paris. This is what I am doing. And I am taking the opportunity to do more than that.

More confessions. When we met this afternoon, I had intended that it should be for the last time. I shouldn't wonder if you didn't guess that.

No need to trample around in the mire and drag out the reasons why. There's only one reason, anyhow. And it's nothing either of us can do anything about—and least of all you, as I'm perceptive enough to appreciate.

Your week away in Paris would have provided a convenient break in the chain, I told myself. Come the week after next, and I could bring about a sharp disassociation. No more phone calls. Just "Hi, Candy!" when we met. An end to it all.

Now I know that I can't do it.

I'm not in love with you. That has to be said. I've never loved anyone in my life—not even myself very much—and I've come to accept that the capacity to love is something they were handing out while I was queuing up for some of the more flashy commodities, like the gift of the gab and a way with dumb animals—particularly dogs. I don't think that you're in love with me, either, indeed it would embarrass me very much if you were.

Why, then, you may very well ask, is this Stanton man unable to make a break with Candida Jeans, a spinster of this parish?

I will tell you, in hard, round, and naked terms.

It's because you are, without doubt, the basically nicest person of either sex whom I've ever met in my life. You exude—did you know it?—a curious, quiet enchantment that affects everyone you meet. People talk about it. Not to your face, because you're a frightened little marmoset who'd run a mile at the mention of it. This is not to say that the quiet enchantment isn't capable of getting tatty round the edges in times of stress (I've got a scar on my arm to prove it— but none of that now), but the way you are has made you an absolute necessity to me. I face up to myself, as I sit here, with a whole sea of Scotch behind me, and realize that I can't manage without this thing you have.

*There's another thing. You must know it—but probably
never give it a thought, though it screams out at you from
every glossy magazine on the bookstalls. You're not possibly
the most beautiful bird in the whole world. But the way
you look, the way you walk, and the way you just stand
and do nothing could probably be proved, experimentally,
to have a discernible therapeutic effect on the eyes. I would
make the wild statement—drunk as I am—that a man in a
situation of progressive blindness would not, could not,
entirely drift into eternal blindness while ever you could be
kept in the range of his vision. Does that sound extravagant?*

*I may not ever possess you, Candida Jeans, spinster of
this parish and updated Helen of Troy; but while ever you're
around, that's where I want to be too.*

*Ring you at your hotel on Tuesday evening at exactly
six o'clock. Will book the call in advance. Be there.*

Dispatched to Paris, France—from Paris Stanton.

The harshness had gone out of the gray day, and had
turned to the silky blueness of night, as she sat there by
the window. The street below was lit up and the stars
were out. Time had gone past.

She added it all up, and it came to this: Jeremy's letter—
setting aside the tipsy extravagances—answered, for the first
time, all she needed to know about his side of their relationship, and it complemented her own wants. He liked having
her around because she was an easy companion with a pliable
disposition, who listened to his amusing talk and laughed
with him. He admired her looks—she'd always known that—
and was proud to be seen around with her. . . .

But not in the work-and-social world he usually inhabited;
Helen of Troy was strictly for new surroundings that they'd
carved out for themselves: quiet restaurants and bars just

outside town, the park in spring blossom, afternoons at the sea.

Why? Was it fear of meeting Sonia?

She took out the concept and looked at it dispassionately. That Jeremy Stanton was a man of normal appetites was something that had never been even slightly difficult for her to accept; in fact, considering the dressing-room set's estimate of his proclivities, his appetites were probably exceptional— and that had never worried her either. The Brighton episode apart, he had never strained their relationship beyond the bounds that she had set down. And the letter showed that he, too, had found something of value in what had grown up between them. If he took other women, it was because they were able to give something that was beyond her to give.

She had never let herself brood about it. Yes, she had— once—on Saturday evening, when she'd discovered his deceit. When she'd decided that he'd chucked her.

Not to think about that. Shut it out.

Concentrate on something else. Sonia . . .

She knew, now, why Sonia had been so bitchy on this Paris trip—bitchy, even for her. While she, Candida, was still delayed at the police station, Sonia had come back and had been handed the letter by Charles ("There's a letter for Miss Jeans. Will she be long?" "Don't worry, I'll give it to her.") She'd recognized the Grave Vale stationery, and opened it.

Why? She'd no reason to guess it was from Jeremy, and even *his* characteristically bad typing couldn't have been sufficiently apparent, from the four lines of address on the envelope, to make the hopeless indiscretion of ripping it open. Strange.

Anyhow, she'd read the letter, and what she had seen

there accounted for her dreadful mood at dinner on Monday evening—and everything that followed.

That wasn't all. Candida felt her skin prickle with the shock of the realization.

The reason for their lateness in finishing work on Tuesday afternoon, in the stonemason's yard—when Sonia quite arbitrarily demanded a reshoot and kept them till well past six—*was so that Candida wouldn't be in the hotel when the phone call came through from Jeremy!*

Was it a current affair? An occasional, casual coupling? Had Jeremy Stanton had Sonia Hammersley and then discarded her?

Whatever the pattern, there was—or had been—something between them. What more likely? They worked together on the same magazine. Sonia was attractive to men, and almost certainly quite promiscuous. Given the personalities of the two people involved, it was almost inevitable that it should have happened at some time or other.

Was she—Candida—jealous?

She decided she was not. Rereading the letter, it was all there: all she had ever asked, or wanted, or was able to accept, from Jeremy Stanton—or from any man.

But Sonia Hammersley's position was quite different. The ruthless acquisitiveness that was going to send her right to the top of her profession would never allow her to accept that any man to whom she'd given herself could write on quite those terms to another woman—particularly to someone whom she regarded, Candida knew, as nothing but a hysterical little cow.

It didn't matter. All that mattered was that she wasn't alone any longer. Jeremy was available, at the far end of a telephone line, to take from her some of the burden of horror. He'd listen, and then tell her what she already knew she had to do; only, his precise reasonableness would make it sound easy.

She drew the blinds, switched on the bedside light and picked up the phone. Charles, the reception clerk, answered, and said he'd attend to it right away, when she asked him to put through a call to England and gave him Jeremy Stanton's phone number.

Charles said he would call her back. She was turning on the bath taps when the ring of the phone sent her running like a bride to her groom.

"Hello. That you, Candy?" It was Hilary Lubbock.

She mouthed something.

"Thank heaven you're back, love. Look, we've got to forget what happened today. I'm really to blame, but I waded into Sonia and nearly had her in tears. Are you listening?"

"Yes."

"Just imagine—tears! You'd never have believed it of our little Sonia, would you? It was my fault, sure, but she never should have been so filthy to you. I told her that neither of us realized what a hell of a strain you've been under since—well, you know. . . .

"The upshot is, love, that Sonia wants to do the big climb-down and reconciliation thing. She's very keen—she really is quite sincere about it, Candy. What she has in mind is a rather special dinner, with dressing up, and drinks before. So shall we all meet up in the downstairs bar in—say—an hour's time?"

It was seven o'clock.

"I'm waiting for a phone call to London," she said. "But I'll be through by then. Yes, I'll be there."

"That's my gal. See you, Candy. And we'll make it like nothing's ever happened."

That's the way it's going to be, she told herself. If Sonia had seen the empty envelope, she would *know*. But she—Candida—would say nothing about it. No recriminations. Just the acceptance that they both knew what had happened. If Sonia was in the mood for reconciliation, she'd be genuinely relieved that there wasn't going to be a scene about the letter. One thing about professional women journalists, they were able to carry off a bad situation, when pushed.

She'd meet them for dinner. By then, she'd feel much better: strengthened by having told Jeremy about the horror that was haunting her. By then, he would have put the whole thing in perspective, and ironed it all out for her. She hoped he'd be his usual six whiskies up to par—and smiled at the thought.

The phone rang again.

"Miss Jeans?" It was Charles. He sounded distraught. "All the lines to London are heavily booked, I'm afraid, and there's a delay on all calls."

"How long?"

"A minimum of six hours."

Six hours meant past midnight.

"Shall I book the call for you around breakfast time in the morning, Miss Jeans?"

"No," she said. "Put me through as soon as you can, and I'll be here in my room from midnight on."

"Right, Miss Jeans. I won't be on duty then, but I'll tell the night porter to be around to take the call and put it straight through to you."

"Thank you, Charles."

The prospect of meeting Sonia Hammersley and Lubbock

without having drawn on Jeremy Stanton's strength prompted her to plead a headache.

But no. She'd go through with it. Come midnight—or soon after—and everything was going to be all right. All she had to do was cling onto that thought.

◀ SEVEN ▶

SHE SAW HERSELF in the glass door of the bar leading off the hotel foyer: white face framed in corkscrew side curls, white Indian silk dress; it seemed to her that she looked like a corpse with a sequined handbag.

The bar had also a street entrance, and a life of its own that was divorced from the hotel: businessmen brought their girl friends, and sometimes their wives, after office hours. They were huddled at tables and crowded at the counter. A few of them eyed Candida appreciatively as she edged her way past the packed chairs.

Sonia Hammersley and Lubbock had a table by the window. The photographer got up and kissed her cheek.

"You look adorable," he said.

"It's her job to look adorable," said Sonia Hammersley. "That's how she makes her bread. What are you going to have, darling?" Her manner was heavily amiable, and Candida registered with dismay that she was more than slightly drunk. She had changed into a simple black dress with an elaborate rhinestone choker collar, and had discarded her heavy glasses for contact lenses that accentuated the staring regard she fixed on Candida.

"I think I'd like a Campari-soda, please."

"Rubbish, my dear. Tonight's on the old firm, and you'll have champagne cocktails and like 'em. Garçon!" She flicked her fingers at a boyish waiter, and made a big thing of squeezing his upper arm. "Set up three more like the last, there's an angel."

Lubbock met Candida's inquiring glance, rolled his eyes, and hunched his shoulders in confirmation. Candida realized that Sonia Hammersley must have filled in the time after getting out of the bath—and perhaps discovering that the letter had gone?—by taking advantage of the room service. How many drinks had she downed since—when was it?—four o'clock? Obviously quite a lot. But they seemed to have improved her mood; she was still molding the young waiter's arm and blatantly flirting with him in her inaccurate and appallingly accented French.

Lubbock took the opportunity to lean over and whisper close to Candida's ear: "Watch your step, duckie. I promise you I had her in splendid mood this afternoon, but something seems to have changed her between then and now. Or maybe it's the drinks. . . ."

"What are you two muttering about?" asked Sonia Hammersley. Her lacquered finger ends still plucking at the sleeve of the waiter's jacket, she was eyeing them aggressively.

"Just small-talk, love," said Lubbock blandly.

"Don't you approve of my hob-nobbing with *les domestiques?*" said Sonia. "Or is it that you're making plans to

push off upstairs and do a little mutual hob-nobbing of your own when you've got rid of me?"

"Sonia, baby, don't be like that." Lubbock eased his chair over and slid his fingers caressingly over her free hand.

"Don't Sonia-baby me, you camera-clicking pouf!" She switched her glance to Candida, and her voice rose. "He is a pouf, you know. You'll be quite safe with darling Hilary, for all his big muscles and butch looks."

Lubbock cut through all that: the sudden, regarding silence of the people at the adjoining tables, Candida's sick embarrassment—and concentrated on placating the girl at his side.

"I can't help me propensities," he said, with good-humored mock humility. "It's all on account of having been brought up by Mummy, after Daddy ran off with me sister. How can you be beastly to a poor boy what was made to wear a lace collar and ringlets right up till, and including, the day he was sent to Eton? I was crucified for being a pouf there, and ever since. Give us a kiss, ducks, and tell me you love me in spite of all."

Sonia laughed, hoarsely and tipsily, and kissed him on the proffered cheek, pulling his head down to her, roughly. "Hilly, you're a bloody lying fool," she said, "and I love you. All men are rotten swine, but you're halfway to being really quite nice."

His muffled voice came from somewhere behind her tousled blonde hair: "I try hard not to be a pouf."

"That you do, darling," said Sonia Hammersley. "And it's really quite pathetic to watch you at it, 'cos you've got two strikes against you. In addition to the lace-collar thing, you're also a prisoner of your ghastly upper-class upbringing. Before England swung and became trendy here, they used to lampoon fellows like you in the Paris music halls: you were the Englishman in the bowler hat who perched at the other end of the tart's sofa, reading the *Times* and pretending she wasn't there. You're a sweet boy, Hilly, but that phantom bowler will always stop you from getting really turned on."

"You turn me on, dear!" Lubbock's face appeared over the top of Sonia Hammersley's head. He made a wild grimace of triumph at Candida, and a V-sign with his fingers. Candida checked an impulse to giggle with relief.

The bad moment was past, and the people at the next tables returned reluctantly to their own affairs. The boy waiter brought drinks, and Candida searched Sonia Hammersley's face over the rim of her champagne glass. She was in a dangerous mood that was lightly overlaid with a thin carapace of alcohol, so that Hilary had been able to jolly her out of the insulting outburst. The drink was not the cause of her mood; it had to be the other thing—the letter.

Lubbock was speaking to her: "Sonia's got something rather special laid on for us tonight, haven't you, love? But she's playing it slightly close to her vest, and won't let on. For my money, it could be anything from a gourmet dinner at the Tour d'Argent to hamburgers at Le Drug. Come on, Sonia honey—give."

Sonia Hammersley smiled secretly in her glass. "No sale," she murmured. "You'll just have to wait and see. But I can promise you it will be all very . . . amusing." The myopic, lensed eyes flickered up and met Candida's, and Candida was disturbingly aware of a shock wave of malice in the glance.

"Well, shall we drink up and move on, gels?" said Lubbock. "It's past eight o'clock and you must both be famished."

Sonia Hammersley's gaze never wavered from Candida

as she replied: "I'm picking up the bill for this evening's entertainment, and we leave when I say, and not until. Order another round of drinks."

I just know, thought Candida, that this is going to be one of the worst evenings of my life. But it will all be over by midnight.

That was the consolation she clung to. No matter what, she would be back in her room by midnight, to take the call to Jeremy.

Sonia directed their taxi to Montmartre, and grumbled all the time that the cabbie—taking them for a trio of clueless tourists—was driving them halfway round Paris to reach the top of the Butte. She paid him off at a corner of the Place du Tertre, short-changed him on his tip, and walked off for the others to follow her. Lubbock slipped the man a couple of coins and tucked Candida's arm in his.

"Chin up, duckie," he said. "It could get worse as the night proceeds—and it probably will."

"I have to be back at the hotel before twelve," she said. "I've booked a call to London."

"I'll get you back," he promised. "Stick it out till then, and leave me to deal with Sonia's antics."

They followed her along the cobbled street; past the drinkers at the café tables, past the artists and their painted canvases. It was nine-thirty, and Paris's loveliest and most disarming tourist trap was at the rich peak of giving of its all. An absurdly full moon in a deep Prussian-blue sky looked benignly down on the old square; on the ridiculously handsome hodgepodge of houses with their crazy roofs and eyeless upper windows; on the crowd scene of strollers and lookers, sitters and drinkers, busy waiters, good painters and bad painters, natives and tourists, young lovers, old lovers—

set there once and for all time as a cast that changed nightly and always remained the same.

"Where's she taking us?" said Candida.

"I think darling Sonia's lost her way," he said. "We may end up at the Tour d'Argent after all, if our luck holds, which I doubt. Trouble, Sonia love?"

Sonia Hammersley had brought a feather stole with her; she flipped the long end of it over her shoulder with a gesture of impatience. "I think the place is down this street," she said, "but I may be wrong. I haven't been here for ages, and all the damn' streets look alike."

"What's it called?" asked Lubbock.

"I can't remember!" she snapped. "If I could, I'd have told that cretin of a driver to drop us there, wouldn't I? It's down here somewhere—come on!" And she set off down a dark street that led from the lighted square, over the far side of Montmartre knoll.

"'Come on,' she says," muttered Lubbock. "It's the Duchess from *Alice in Wonderland* all over again. Come on, Candy, before our gourmet dinner's metamorphosed into a hamburger after all."

Their goal—signaled by a triumphant cry from their guide—was a row of lighted windows halfway down the steeply sloping street. The building was on a corner. Its end—and perhaps the whole line of tall hovels to which it was joined—was shored up by a pair of wooden buttresses. There was an illuminated sign over the arched doorway:

CHEZ MARTHE

"After the build-up," said Hilary Lubbock *sotto voce*, "Marthe had better keep a good table."

Candida had been walking like a somnambulist, and willing herself to be back in her hotel room. She focused on the sign, but before it really made any sense to her they were inside; in a crowded, overheated gloom, and a pretty Algerian girl was taking her coat.

"We'll have one at the bar while I fix a table," said Sonia.

The bar ran along one side, divided from the dining space by a low screen and a row of plaster pillars. There was nowhere to sit and no space at the bar. Lubbock eased them through the throng to a small area of standing room by one of the pillars, and Candida sagged thankfully against it.

"Full marks for optimism," said Lubbock, "if you imagine we're going to get a meal here tonight. What would you both like to drink?"

"Leave all that to me," said Sonia Hammersley, and she elbowed away from them, toward the bar.

"This will be worth watching," said Lubbock. "She's going to beard the management. By Jove, yes. That's probably Chez Marthe *soi-même*. Golly, what a corker!"

Sonia had joined a group at the far end of the bar that was dominated by a tall brunette in deep red, who turned when Sonia addressed her and gracefully inclined her sable head to listen. Her face was a deeply tanned mask of utter impassivity. Only the berry-black eyes (Gypsy? Jewish?), thought Candida, were alive: they worked right over the face and figure of the woman who was speaking to her; narrowing and flaring wide in turn, in response to the things she was being told. She made no reply, but only lifted a long cigar to her lips and drew deeply.

"I don't think our little Sonia's getting to first base with Madame Marthe," said Lubbock. "But, no—I'm wrong. . . ."

The splendid face was suddenly animated by an expression of delighted recollection. Sonia Hammersley was drawn against the magnificent prow of bosom and kissed full on the lips. Now the woman was introducing her to her companions, and one of them—a Eurasian girl whose face could have been carved out of sandalwood—also leaned forward to kiss the newcomer.

"We're in," said Lubbock.

Sonia Hammersley was talking again, and gesturing back toward them. Candida saw the Gypsy eyes pan toward her across the smoke-ladened dimness, and felt suddenly alarmed. The woman laughed and said something to the Eurasian, who looked toward Candida and smiled.

Sonia was back a few moments later. Something in her manner sharpened the unease that had nagged at Candida since she met the stare of the woman in red.

"They're laying an extra table for us, and we can have our drinks there. We'll have time to eat before the cabaret, too."

The Algerian waiters led the way across the crowded dining space, a table held on high above them, and napery draped over their shoulders. They put the table at the edge of the small dance floor, so that it jutted out like a peninsula.

"Allowing that the dancing girls are going to be falling all over us, this is still pretty good," said Lubbock. "How did you put the Indian sign on that statuesque dyke?"

"I came here during the spring collections a couple of years back. This was when Nicky Randall was managing editor of *Focal*, and expense accounts were just a joke. I came over to Paris with no less than three photographers and their assistants, and five models. Nicky had recommended this place, so I brought them here one night, the whole boiling, and we had a ball. Marthe took a little prodding, but she remembered me in the end—the one who footed the enormous bill." She laid a hand on Candida's. "Darling, you look like Little Orphan Annie in a decline. One just shouldn't have brought you out after the frightful day you've had, but I'm sure you'll respond to nourishment." She took a menu from one of the hovering waiters and spread it out between them like a hymn sheet. "Now, let's choose together, should we?"

Candida was not hungry, and mistrusted Sonia's new switch of mood, but she seconded the other's choice of soufflé de turbot and poulet flambé à l'armagnac. Hilary Lubbock said he'd go along with all that.

All in all, the meal went off well. Lubbock slipped easily from one light-weight monologue to another. Candida ate more than she would have believed possible, and told herself that she was going to survive the evening quite happily. Sonia Hammersley moved the food about on her plate, but barely took a mouthful; she drank the lion's share of a bottle of Montrachet, and called for another.

They were at the coffee stage when a five-piece band shuffled out from behind a curtain, took their places on a dais above the dance floor, and struck up an extended, wavering chord.

"Bring on the dancing girls," grinned Lubbock.

The dancing girls were obvious twin sisters: healthy peasant girls, who did a semigymnastic dance to within a hairbreadth of their table, wafting them with the scent of cheap talcum powder and patchouli. They were followed by a starveling of a man dressed as a tramp, who opened his act by swallowing a string of razor blades.

"The entertainment lags a long way behind the cuisine, which is excellent," said Lubbock.

Candida stole a glance at her watch: ten-thirty. That left about an hour before she had to leave; and she hoped that Sonia wouldn't make any fuss about it.

She looked up, and saw that Sonia Hammersley was

staring at her. She assembled a nervous smile, but it met with no response; the other switched her gaze to the wine bottle and refilled her own glass. Her hand was trembling.

The tramp-illusionist finished his turn and bowed his way out. The lights dimmed, and a clash of cymbals gave the lead-in to reedy oriental-style music. Immediately, Candida was aware of a stir of excitement in the audience. The people at the bar crowded into the gangway, and the diners at the rearmost tables got to their feet. There was a general scraping of chairs and a readjustment of viewpoints; pale disks of faces separated out in the gloom and completely walled in the semicircle of the small dance floor. From where Candida was sitting, the effect was claustrophobic.

"This must be the high spot," said Lubbock.

It was the Eurasian girl who had been at the bar with Madame Marthe. She made her entrance in a green spotlight that picked out only the upper part of her torso, nude under drapes of swaying chiffon. She stayed at the edge of the floor, making liquid movements with her hands and arms in time to the music; then moved forward, pirouetting slowly, to the middle of the floor.

The loom of the moving spotlight threw Lubbock's profile into sharp silhouette; he was staring at the dancer and grinning like a mischievous schoolboy. Candida stifled a yawn. It was hot and airless in the overcrowded room.

The spotlight changed color to cerise, and widened to take in the whole of the girl's body. She was barefoot, with harem trousers, and a heavy sash encircled her hips.

Suddenly—she was less than two yards away from Candida, who was breathing her heavy scent—the girl brought the music to a stop by clapping her hands above her head. She stayed posed like that, arms raised, for a full half-minute. Then her head began to weave from side to side, eyes closed. The second figure of the dance began in silence, till the thin notes of a pipe took up the rhythmic movements of the girl's head, and she increased the tempo, bringing her arms and shoulders and the whole of the upper part of her body into play.

Another pipe, shriller and louder, added a counterpoint.

And one end of the thing coiled about the dancer's hips—the thing that Candida had mistakenly supposed to be a richly embroidered sash—fell away to one side, and then rose toward the girl's snapping fingers. Through the first mists of faintness, Candida saw the flickering tongue and the eyes like drowned seed pearls; then she met the draining away of blood from her brain by bowing her head in her hands. Lubbock's hand was on her shoulder the same instant.

"What's up, love—do snakes upset you?"

She froze, squeezing him out of her consciousness, along with everything else. The important thing was not to pass out; not completely to lose the power over one's body, so that mind and body toppled. It could only be done alone; any contact with sounds and feelings from outside increased the spinning vertigo.

Everything—the sounds and the smells—receded from her, and the only tactile thing was the pressure of her own fingers against her eyeballs. Time went past.

It was a long journey back to reality: the reality of what was going on beyond the eyelids and fingers that guarded her in.

Her first thought was to flight. She tested the notion of rising to her feet and rushing blindly in any direction; but remembered the claustrophobic arc of pale faces that hemmed her in—and the horror that was moving about in the tiny space where she was sitting. Stay where you are. Wait—and let it go away.

The music was coming to a crescendo. Hilary Lubbock had long since stopped plucking at her shoulder. She thought she could hear the rhythmic drumming of the girl's bare feet, and they seemed blessedly far away. There was another sound: it could have been someone trying to smother a fit of laughter —but it wasn't important. Only the end was important.

She waited for the end, anticipating it. The final crescendo; a cymbal clash; a piping coda; more cymbals. End. Applause. Wait.

Now—she opened her eyes.

The snake's shrunken, old-man's head was close up in front of her face, held there at the full extent of the Eurasian girl's arm. And the girl's head was superimposed above the other, so that two pairs of eyes were looking down at her. Mockery and drowned seed pearls.

She screamed when the tongue flickered out of the gummy mouth toward her; but the sound of it was lost in general laughter and a renewal of the applause. The Eurasian girl pulled a funny face at her, then backed away, gathering up the snake's coils and bowing to her audience.

All the lights went up, and taped beat music brought some couples crowding onto the dance floor. The show was over, and the laughing stopped. But not all the laughing.

"Cut it out, Sonia, for God's sake!" said Lubbock.

Sonia Hammersley was sagged in her chair in a paroxysm of giggling, streaming-eyed and with trails of spittle running from the corners of her mouth. No one was watching them, and no one noticed when Hilary Lubbock leaned across and smacked her sharply across one cheek, snuffing out the fit of hysterics like a candle flame.

The wine bottle at her elbow was empty. Her short-sighted eyes narrowed to focus on Candida.

"You make me laugh," she said. "Jeremy and I—we laugh about you all the time, you silly little bitch."

Lubbock cut in: "Sonia, you simply mustn't . . ."

"Shut up!" she snapped, getting to her feet and wrapping her stole about her, still staring down at Candida. "Jeremy's told me everything about you, you know. Don't think there's anything at all I don't know about you."

She left them then, walking unsteadily through the maze of tables toward the exit.

"Socked me with the bill," said Lubbock. "Cheap at the price, I suppose, to see the back of her for the evening."

They went out together soon after, and Candida saw the flaxen-haired young man who had driven Haquin's car. He was sitting at a corner of the bar, and their eyes met in the mirror beyond.

He turned and gave her a pleasant smile and a nod.

◀ EIGHT ▶

"So she set it up deliberately tonight," said Hilary Lubbock, "because she knew about you and this snake thing—she had it first hand from old Jerry Stanton. Well, I'm damned."

"Yes," said Candida.

They were back in the Place du Tertre, where Lubbock had persuaded her to join him in a coffee before they went to look for a taxi. They sat under the fairy-lit lime trees, and the night air was clean and sharp. She was finding it strangely easy to confide in him.

"I've had it all my life, or as long as I can remember," she said. "It gave me—still gives me—a horrifying jolt even to turn over the pages of a book and see a photograph of a snake. It's as if the real thing were lying there. I couldn't bring myself to touch the page where it was printed."

"And you told Stanton about this?"

"Yes. No one else. I even hid it from Mummy. But, you see, Jeremy has this thing about the zoo."

"I know. When he was a kid he wanted to be a vet."

"Monkeys are his special delight, but he can gaze at almost any animal for hours, no matter how revolting. Quite soon there was the question of going into the reptile house, so I had to tell him. And, being Jeremy, he had to know the lot. He said it was a phobia and that it could be cured by some kind of therapy. I'd no idea you knew him quite well, Hilary."

"Known him for ages," said Lubbock. "When I came down from Oxford and decided photography was my thing, he'd just finished art college. We were both hard up, and shared a flat for about a year."

"He never talks about you," said Candida.

Lubbock pulled a wry mouth. "I'm not surprised. We managed to get on each other's nerves by the end of that year. Come to that, he's never spoken of you, either."

"Except to Sonia," she said. "And she claims to know everything there is to know."

"The snake phobia apart," said Lubbock, "would she be likely to know anything that you wouldn't wish to be known?"

She nodded. "It's possible."

"How long's the affair been going on between you and Jerry Stanton? Not that it's any of my business."

"Since last August. Only—what we have going isn't an affair."

"I see. And our little Sonia—you've only just found out what she had going with Stanton?"

"Today," she said, "I found a letter from Jeremy, posted to me at the hotel, that she'd opened and kept to herself. I realize now that she must have known about Jeremy and me to have done that. And she could only have heard it from him."

"True enough," said Lubbock. "He certainly kept you

under wraps. But, then, you never mixed with the whoopee set, have you? And Stanton's bright enough not to have dragged you into it with him."

"Why do you say that—why should he keep me apart?" He looked at her over the rim of his coffee cup.

"Because you might get a taste for the whoopee life," he said. "Meet socially a lot of folks whom you've so far only known in the work situation. Let down your hair a little. Dish the dirt with the rest of the girls . . ."—he grinned— ". . . in the whoopee situation, Stanton might have lost you to someone else long before now. Me, for instance."

"A portrait sketch of the beautiful young lady?" They had noticed the man in the black slouch hat and cape moving from table to table with his sketchbook. He was middle-aged, smooth, and aggressively Bohemian.

"I don't think the beautiful young lady's very keen," said Lubbock.

The Bohemian made a painterly gesture around Candida's head. "She is an inspiration," he breathed. "If you will not give me a commission to sketch her, I ask only to be allowed to do it for love of beauty."

Lubbock laughed. "With a pitch like that, you deserve the job. We've got five minutes to spare, haven't we, Candy? . . .

"Candy, love, is anything the matter? You look as if you've seen a ghost."

She shook her head. "It's nothing."

But there was something. The Bohemian's manner, his plump white hands, and the reek of stale spirits that he had wafted over her, had set in motion a chain of association that —coupled with Hilary Lubbock's recent inquisition—brought a long-suppressed memory tumbling out of her past.

The hard-won reappraisal from Mummy had its full flowering in the Indian summer of her thirteenth year, and Candida

—while never relaxing her anxious efforts—was contented with her slim victory.

It was easy, now, to accept that her love for Mummy must never be expressed in terms of touching and kissing; already, the young girl was herself cauterized against fleshly contact. To be with her mother, sitting opposite her in the lacy shade of the sitting room and quietly talking over the low-keyed happenings of their daily lives; to know that Mummy was proud of her, and seemed to consider her washed clean of her father's dirt—these things were enough. The limits had been set up, and there was only dirt on the other side. The recurring image of Mlle. Rosen taking off her pebble glasses to kiss her photograph made Candida feel physically sick, and she thrust it out of her mind whenever it appeared.

The summer of that year—her first term at her public school—was protracted through a languorous October of warm stillness and sun-browned arms, when Uncle Bernard was able to drive them for evening picnics at a quiet reach of the River Trent. He fished for roach, and Mummy read a book, while Candida changed in the car and swam across the river, to where the solid wall of tall trees on the far bank were blackly mirrored in the slow-moving water. Once, she stayed in too long: the cold meat and salad was already laid out and the coffee poured. Candida had no time to change out of her wet costume, so she had her supper with a towel draped over her shoulders; shivering with cold, and hunching her back when she saw—almost for the first time ever, and with hideous embarrassment—how the wet costume mercilessly outlined the structure of her growing bosom, and the others must surely have noticed it, too, mustn't they?

The Indian summer—and everything else—ended one Thursday evening.

Mummy had signed up to attend a winter course of lectures

on art appreciation at the Women's Institute on Thursday evenings. The first lecture came on a day when the first morning frost touched the back lawn of St. Aubyn; by the time Mummy had left at seven o'clock, wind and rain were rattling the curtained windows of the living room, and Candida was curled up in an armchair before the fire with Wissie as a bookrest for her Latin grammar.

She never heard a car coming up the drive; only the chimes of the front door bell.

It was Uncle Bernard—there was no mistaking the outline of his homburg hat in the lighted porch beyond the leaded panes of the door. Candida was still muttering the imperfect subjunctive of the verb *audire* when she opened it to him.

"Good grief! What a night!" He took off his hat and shook away the drops onto the mat.

She shut the door, and ruefully decided to leave her homework for bedtime.

"Mummy's out—gone to the lecture. Would you like a cup of coffee, Uncle Bernard?"

He'd forgotten about the art-appreciation lectures, and apologized for disturbing her homework. They sipped their coffee, and Candida tucked her stockinged feet beneath her on the sofa; he had taken her armchair by the fire. Uncle Bernard was not a demanding conversationalist, and tonight he seemed content to bumble on without pausing for her replies. She resigned herself to an hour of gentle boredom, and let her attention wander back to the intricacies of the imperfect subjunctive.

The alien smell was the thin edge of the warning that Uncle Bernard was different from usual that night; it had gently prickled her nostrils when she re-entered the room with the coffee tray, but she had put it down to the smoke from the first, unaccustomed fire of winter; ten minutes later, it was more pervasive—and it seemed to come from the man in the armchair.

Drink! Apart from an occasional sherry, Mummy never drank or kept drink in the house—and certainly not spirits. Yet, from somewhere in her life—perhaps while passing the open door of a public house—Candida had a perfect recollection of that sweet, cloying smell that kept coming at her, across the warm room.

Uncle Bernard had been drinking. Then was he drunk? Candida decided that this might be so.

". . . yes, a delightful room," he was saying. "Always liked it. Reflects your mother's personality. A lonely old widower like myself . . ."—his eyes swiveled to meet Candida's, and they were surely red-rimmed—". . . lonely old widower. Been a home to me. And the two of you've been like family, Candida."

She was mistaken. It was quite stupid of her. Now he had come over and joined her on the sofa, plumping down heavily and grinning at her the way he always did. But he certainly had been drinking; the fumes made her feel quite sick. She pulled her serge uniform skirt down over her bent knees, wriggled her legs further out of sight, and willed him to go home.

"How are you getting on at school—lots of homework?" She made a *moue*. "Latin tonight."

"Let's have a look at your book. I used to be very hot at the old Latin."

To humor him, she got up and crossed over to where the Latin grammar was lying by the armchair; stooping to pick it up, she saw a movement from the corner of her eye. When she turned round, he was sitting splay-legged and unbuttoned —grinning across at her.

"How's that, then?" When he spoke, a trickle of spittle ran from the corner of his mouth.

He caught her by the waist halfway to the door, and her scream was taken up by the wild howl of the cat as it got between their feet. Uncle Bernard kicked at the animal's underbelly and sent it cartwheeling across the room, where it slammed against the far wall and lay retching.

Candida tried to turn the door handle, but he pulled her back; her fingers scrabbled and lost it.

"Let me go—please!"

The fire seemed to have gone out of him. Still holding her round the waist from behind, he was pleading with her.

"Look—it was all a mistake. Impulse of the moment. I don't know what came over me. Please—calm down. Let's forget the whole rotten business."

She drew in a lungful of his reeking breath, and kicked back with her stockinged heels.

"Candy, love—you've *got* to forget it. For *all* our sakes!"

She twisted her body, and one of his hands slipped from her waist; it found a new purchase in the buttoning of her school blouse when she broke free and, turning, raked his screaming face with her fingernails.

And then she was out of Mummy's cosy living room, and out of the front door, in the night of rain and wind.

It was not even a competent sketch, for all the Bohemian's theatrical posturings; but merely a mannered attempt at Candida's profile, and not at all a good likeness. Lubbock paid him off, settled for the coffee, and they set off down the steep street of steps, with all Paris alight below them. It was just past eleven-fifteen.

"He's ringing you around midnight?" asked Lubbock.

"I'm ringing him," she said, and she explained about the phone call that Jeremy Stanton had arranged in the letter.

"That conniving baggage," said Lubbock. "That's why she had us on overtime, eh? Candy, she's really put the knife into you while we've been here. I thought it was just her general bitchiness. Like the time she sent that crazy woman with your make-up bag—a deliberate attempt to put a gratuitous scare into you—but there's been more to it than that. La Sonia is jealous, and a woman scorned, I shouldn't wonder."

"I don't know anything about her affair with Jeremy," said Candida. "Or when it happened—except that some of it's obviously happened since I've known Jeremy."

"Yes. And I'd say, offhand, that he's recently chucked her, which accounts for the way she's been carrying on, up to and including the grotesque scene she stage-managed tonight. By the way"—he touched her arm—"have you got over that now?"

"I nearly passed out in that place when I saw—it," she said. "It happened once before in my life, when I was a child. We were being taken for a school walk in some woods, and one of the girls found an adder. I fainted at the sight of it. I told Jeremy about it."

Their eyes met, and she looked away. They had reached the bottom of the steps, and Lubbock did not comment again till they had come to the top of the next flight.

"I think," he said, "that my old chum and former flatmate has been telling a hell of a lot too many tales out of school, and to a very bad class of person."

They found a taxi quite easily in the boulevard. Now they were minutes from the hotel, and she was able to sit back and relax. In half an hour, or less, she would have laid all her problems in front of Jeremy. Reassured by the things he had said about her in his letter—about his need for her—she knew that he wouldn't jib at accepting the load of her troubles. Sonia Hammersley—whatever she'd been to him, and whatever private things he'd let slip to her—meant nothing alongside the things he'd said in the letter.

She could forgive him. She could even find the compassion to forgive Sonia Hammersley.

"Just one thing I'd like to ask, but tell me to mind my own business, if you feel that way," said Lubbock.

"Go on," she said.

"Jerry Stanton's a very attractive chap," he said. "Doesn't attract me personally, but then I once lived with him, and close proximity with my fellow men is something I've never come to terms with ever since I was sent away to boarding school at the age of eight. But I'd say he's an attractive chap. Right?"

"Yes."

"You think so, and I think so, and obviously a lot of other people think so—including dear Sonia. Six foot of creamy muscle topped off with a charming smile. What I want to ask you is this, Candy: Do you have any long-term plans that include Jerry Stanton?"

"Marriage? You mean, has he asked me to marry him?"

"Candy, I know—but don't ask me how I know—that he hasn't asked you to marry him. What I'm asking is, do you have any other quasipermanent connection in mind? Up to and including, say, giving him your lifelong devotion, or going to live with him, or something."

The floodlit bulk of the Madeleine was ahead. She smiled toward it.

"Jeremy gives me something that I've never known before," she said quietly. "A sort of confidence in myself. A freedom from feelings that have upset me for almost as long as I can remember—guilt feelings, sensations of inadequacy. I don't know if I love him. I mayn't even be sufficiently complete as a woman completely to love a man. And he's not in love with me. But, while things remain as they are between us, I can't see any end to it. Does that answer your question?"

"Yes," he said. He squeezed her hand. "And it makes me feel a hell of a lot better about you, Candy."

There was no one in the hotel foyer but the night porter, a mousy old man in a long navy-blue apron, who had to peer very closely at the numbers on their key tags to check that he was giving out the right ones. Despite Candida's doubts, however, he displayed a complete knowledge of the forthcoming call to London. Charles had instructed him most carefully, he said. As soon as the exchange rang through at midnight or thereabouts, he would immediately connect the call with Mam'selle Jeans in Room 46. As if further to test the old fellow's competence, Lubbock gave him a complicated set of instructions regarding times of calling in the morning, with coffee or tea, and various newspapers, for the three members of the party. The night porter wrote it all down right first time.

Lubbock also checked to see if Sonia Hammersley was in. She was. They said good night to the old man and got into the lift.

"I don't quite know how we'll handle little Sonia to-morrow," he said. "I really think things have got to a pass when one should make some kind of formal complaint to her managing editor—but I don't suppose we ever shall. One con-solation: she's going to have the mother and father of all hangovers in the morning, and that'll make her tractable!"

They parted outside her door. He asked her to give his

kind regards to Jeremy Stanton; she said that she would, and kissed his cheek.

She shut the door behind her; went straight into the bathroom and turned on the lights. When she laid her wristwatch on the ledge above the washbasin it said ten to twelve.

She undressed in the bathroom and put on the toweling robe provided by the hotel, scooped up her hair under a chiffon band, and slapped a bobble of cold cream on her nose, chin, and each cheek. Rub well in.

(Tissues—in case the phone rings first, with me all greased up.)

The tissues were in the mirror-fronted cabinet before her. She opened the door, and the mirrored rectangle gave her a quick, panning glimpse of one side of the bathroom, the open door, and the darkened room beyond, with the pale bulk of the bed at the far end.

The message she received was of a very low key of impression, and reached her consciousness so slowly that her hand had closed round the pack of tissues, before it froze.

Very slowly—without turning her head toward the door —she closed the cabinet till the bedroom and what lay there was reflected there again. And she felt the hairs at the back of her neck stiffen and rise, one by one.

There was a man lying in her bed.

The silhouette of his head was quite discernible against the pillowcase, and the shape of his body rose above the flat plane of the bed.

Horror, alarm, indignation, the need for flight—these were all jockeying for a place in her mind as she reached round the angle of the door and snapped on the main bedroom lights.

"*Jeremy!*"

That was the first, unbelievable thought that came to her then: that Jeremy Stanton was lying asleep in her bed.

Asleep and ill—for he was deathly pale, and there were days of stubble on his chin and around his open mouth.

It was only when she spoke to him, to waken him; touched the shoulder and chest and found that they yielded and were only made of a rolled-up bolster, that she pulled back the sheets.

The severed head of Jeremy Stanton was cradled in the hollow of the pillow. There were a few frayed strands of tissue at the hacked-off neck, near where the sheet was lightly dabbled with watery blood.

◀ NINE ▶

At seventeen minutes past twelve, the phone buzzer brought the night porter from the kitchen, where he had been making himself a cup of coffee. An operator of the European service informed him that there was no reply from the London number that had been booked for a call by Miss C. Jeans, and were there any further instructions? The night porter called Room 46, and when no one answered, he told the European operator that he would ring her back later when he had made inquiries.

It was the pique of the elderly—for he had been well aware that both Candida and Lubbock had been doubtful about his ability to cope with the rudimentary hotel switchboard—that sent him upstairs in the lift, to wake the young Englishwoman and give her the news.

There was no answer to his knock. He found the door both unlocked and ajar.

What he found lying on the pillow of the bed did not

cause him any particularly strong mental anguish, beyond a shock that sent his old heart thudding. His father had been a horse butcher in Dieppe, and he had seen something of war besides.

He sat down and thought out the priorities. This done, he first called the hotel manager—as a good company man—told him what had happened, and said that he would ring the police.

In the event, the flaxen-haired Inspector Martin was pounding on the plate-glass front door before the night porter had got down to the foyer again.

Martin and two others had received the alarm call in a car at the corner of the square from which they were watching the hotel. And Superintendent Haquin was already on his way—summoned from his bachelor bed in a flat in the Eleventh Arrondissement, where he had laid his head—much against his better judgment—to attempt what would have been his first consecutive night's sleep since the arrival in Paris of Candida Jeans.

"But she got away, Martin. You shouldn't have let her get away. Not after all the trouble we've taken to keep close surveillance on her for the last three days and nights."

A rebuke from Haquin was doubly to be dreaded on account of the deep gloom into which minor failures of operation always plunged him. He sat now, in the hotel manager's office they had been lent; craggy face drained with sleeplessness, hooded eyes sorrowful. There was no acrimony in his voice; Martin would have felt better if there had been.

"She went out the back way, Chief. That's clear. This would have been any time between, say, five to twelve and twelve-fifteen, when the night porter was moving around, doing various chores in the foyer, the kitchen and the store cupboard. At the far end of the foyer is a door into a yard that's always kept open, to conform with fire regulations. The yard leads straight out into the back alley."

"The alert's gone out?"

"Yes, Chief. Every patrol vehicle, every officer on the beat, has her description. It's hardly possible that she won't be picked up before morning."

The old night porter came in with a tray holding a cup of coffee and a bottle of lager. He had found time and opportunity, somehow, to put on war medals to grace the occasion, and he stood to attention after he had put down the tray on the manager's desk.

"Thank you," murmured Haquin, picking up the lager.

"Not a very pleasant case for you, sir," said the night porter. "Head without a body."

"No, it isn't," growled Haquin.

Martin picked up his coffee.

"At least it's established that the fellow's dead, Chief," he said lightly. "There was a time, in the beginning, when it was theoretically possible that he was alive and walking round, minus odd pieces of his body, like some ghoul in a cheap movie."

The young sergeant met his supervisor's eyes, and a deep crimson flush spread over his guileless face—as he fought to keep his gaze from dropping to Haquin's aluminum right leg.

The late-night news cinema was warm, and smelled of pine disinfectant. The auditorium was half empty. She sat toward the rear, at a gangway seat. They were showing a Donald Duck cartoon. She was huddled low in her seat, her coat spread across her shoulders, fingers pressed against her lips, eyes closed.

I am destruction, she thought. It began with childhood and

it's gone on ever since. Everyone I touch is soiled, just like Mummy said.

She dared to take her fingers from her lips, risking that the soundless scream they had been imprisoning might burst out in a great noise and betray her; and she looked down at her hands, pale in the gloom.

I destroy everyone I touch. Last of all came Jeremy Stanton, who had a way with monkeys and laughed about sin.

The film ended with a thin pattering of applause, and the lights came up. A taped voice announced that ice cream and chocolate would be on sale during the interval. Music came from behind the drawn curtains. She closed her eyes again and shrank lower in her seat.

Try to think the whole thing through. Plenty of time; no need to make any decisions yet, with the whole long night ahead. How had it all begun?

With Mlle. Rosen, of course.

A slight straining of recollection, and the pale face assembled itself in her mind. Muted violins were playing a current French pop number, but through the music she seemed to hear again the voice of Mlle. Rosen: soft and encouraging, with overtones of a strange longing. The thin hand was resting on her shoulder again, and the myopic eyes gazing down into hers. Strawberries and cream cakes for tea. If only Mlle. Rosen wasn't so plain, and didn't smell ever so slightly of perspiration. It was nice, though, to be liked very much by someone; curiously pleasurable to make the effort to be specifically sweet in return, even if it was obvious that the silly creature had a crush on you.

It was my fault, all my fault. Just like Mummy said, I encouraged that pathetic creature and led her on. . . .

The strident blare of a *paso doble* jerked Candida to awareness of her surroundings again, and she opened her eyes. The curtains were peeling open at the beginning of a pictorial news feature. The house lights were dimming. Also, she was no longer isolated.

Someone was sitting beside her: someone who must have moved very quietly, or he—it was a man—would have broken into her thoughts and disturbed her. Another thing: he had passed along an entire row of empty seats, in order to be next to her.

Alarmed, she gathered up her coat about her shoulders to leave; was tensing herself to move, when his hand reached out and took hers, and his face came close to her cheek, mouthing false endearments.

She broke from his grasp and ran down the aisle, past the giant figures on the glaring screen; out of a door that yielded instantly to her touch and delivered her onto the thronged, lit-up pavement again.

Sonia Hammersley and Hilary Lubbock were, naturally, awakened. Lubbock was asked to make a formal identification of the head in Room 46; the gruesome exhibit was arranged in the bed with some delicacy, and may not have caused him a lot of anguish. In any event, he did not show it when he was brought down to see Haquin in the manager's office.

The inspector and his assistant were seated side by side at the desk, with an open cardboard portfolio in front of them. Martin got up when Lubbock was shown in by a uniformed officer, and he put a chair in place at the front of the desk.

"Please sit down, Mr. Lubbock," said Haquin. "There are just a few points I should like to settle with you. First, you can confirm that you recognized the features of Jeremy Stanton, who I understand, was well known to you?"

"Yes. It's Stanton all right." Lubbock was wearing his cord battledress over a turtle-neck sweater. A night's stubble lay on his chin, and his eyes were strained.

"When did you see him last, the deceased man?"

Lubbock thought for a while. "Last Tuesday fortnight," he said. "Yes. I can pinpoint it quite definitely, because I had to go to a *Focal* editorial meeting at Grave Vale Press, about the Black Look assignment."

"And Stanton was there?"

"Of course—as art director. He showed me the dummy layouts, giving me a rough idea of his intentions about the feature. Sort of whistled a tune for me to orchestrate."

"Was Miss Jeans there, at this editorial meeting?"

"Oh, no. Models are never brought into the thinking end of the job. Not one in a thousand would have anything to contribute."

"I see." Haquin was making brief notations, in pencil, in the margin of a sheet of typescript. He looked up. "Talking of models, Mr. Lubbock, I wonder if you can supply the answer to something that's been puzzling me about Miss Jeans. To me, she seems a reserved, rather naïve girl who has had a somewhat sheltered upbringing. How would such a girl get into a glamorous occupation like fashion modeling in the first place—and how remain so naïve?"

"I believe she started quite a few years ago as a child model," said Lubbock. "Probably recruited from some genteel little Saturday-morning dancing class. For her, it was only a step from there to the big time. It's one of the classic and least painful routes for a girl who's really outstanding. With her kind of looks she could make it and stay comparatively naïve."

"Thank you," said Haquin. "Now—to revert to the editorial meeting—did you see Stanton after that occasion?"

"No."

"You didn't visit him at his flat."

"No."

Haquin's head remained bowed over the typescript as he asked the next question; but Martin's eyes were on Lubbock.

"This flat. It is, is it not, the same one that you shared in —let me see—nineteen sixty-five?"

"Yes. Why—yes."

Haquin smiled. "You seem surprised that I should have this piece of information, Mr. Lubbock."

Hilary Lubbock hunched his shoulders and made no comment.

"Do you still have the key to the flat?"

"Do I still have the key?" Lubbock scratched his jaw. "Do you know, I think I still have, somewhere. You see, I didn't leave overnight, but moved into a studio flat of my own by easy stages. I actually went back to sleep at Stanton's while my place was being painted out. Then there were things like my laundry to collect. Yes, I think I still have that key somewhere. But I'd be hard put to lay my hands on it."

"So you didn't visit Stanton, at his flat, at any time after the editorial meeting?"

"I've just said *no!*" snapped Lubbock.

Haquin sat back and eyed the photographer mildly.

"Some time tomorrow morning, Mr. Lubbock," he said, "some of my esteemed colleagues from Scotland Yard will be here in Paris. If I seem to press you on this last point, it is simply because they will certainly do the same. And much more forcibly than I, whose jurisdiction in this case is somewhat limited."

"I'm sorry, Superintendent," said Lubbock. "Yes, I confirm that I didn't see Stanton after the meeting, at his flat or anywhere else."

"Thank you, Mr. Lubbock. Next question—did you know of Stanton's affair with Miss Jeans?"

A moment's silence.

"You really do know quite a lot, don't you, Superintendent?" said Lubbock gravely.

"Yes, Mr. Lubbock, we do."

Hilary Lubbock nodded, and said: "I knew nothing about their relationship till last evening. We went out to dinner, the three of us. . . ."

"There was a quarrel," interjected Haquin. "Or was it simply that Miss Hammersley made herself objectionable because she had recently learned of Miss Jean's relationship with Stanton, and was jealous?"

"You have it all pat," said Lubbock, flatly. "Yes, it happened more or less like that."

"Miss Hammersley was jealous."

"Yes."

"You were jealous, perhaps, Mr. Lubbock?" Haquin put the question slowly and deliberately, and was amused to see how easily the big photographer could be made to blush.

"Of Stanton? No, not really."

"But you admire Miss Jeans?"

Hilary Lubbock drove his clenched fist into the palm of his other hand, and repeated the action three more times. He got slowly to his feet and went over to the fireplace, over which hung a steel engraving of Napoleon reviewing his troops. From the back view, he put Haquin in mind of a big tired bear.

"Where is she, Superintendent?" he asked without turning round.

"Somewhere in Paris. We shall find her, never fear."

"She isn't going to do any harm to herself?"

"Not if we find her first. As we shall."

Lubbock nodded, and turned round.

"It really does have no bearing on your inquiries, Superintendent," he said, "but, yes, I do admire Candida Jeans—as you put it"—he drew a very deep breath—"and when all this frightful business is over, I'm going to marry her—if she'll have me."

"I appreciate the confidence, m'sieur," said Haquin with a touch of prim formality. And then: "You were not jealous of Stanton? It didn't occur to you that he might have had plans to marry Miss Jeans himself, perhaps?"

Lubbock shook his head. Slowly and deliberately.

"It could never have happened, Superintendent."

"Why?"

"Because Stanton was a queer."

She had left the boulevard; had wandered into a residential district formed by half a dozen quiet streets that were not too brightly lit but not so dark as to invite prowlers; a district of good-class apartment blocks and a couple of small restaurants. The restaurants were closed, but there were still a few people about—and none of them took the slightest notice of the girl with the coat over her shoulders, who walked swiftly, head down, as if she was actually going somewhere.

I may have all night, she thought. No one will go into the room till morning, surely, when I don't show up for breakfast. Or, perhaps, someone has already gone into the room. Did I leave the door unlocked?

If someone's been in the room already, they'll be looking for me by now.

They mustn't find me. Not till I've had time to think this thing right through.

So I must keep on walking, and pray that I won't be seen. By morning, I shall have decided what I must do.

She rounded a corner, and there was the brightly lit boulevard with the moving traffic and the strolling late-night walkers. She turned and walked back the way she had come.

Mlle. Rosen . . .

She said the name in time to her own footfalls on the pavement, and took great care not to step on the cracks between the flagstones.

It was a Thursday. They had had tea—or, rather, Mlle. Rosen had sat and watched Candida eating her strawberries, watched with private self-gratification—and now Candida was reading aloud from *Letters de mon Moulin;* sitting at the table with the open book between her fingers, with the teacher perched on the arm of an easy chair, looking over her shoulder. Now and then, Mlle. Rosen would softly interrupt her, correcting her accent and cadence. All the time, she was very close, and Candida was aware of her breathing —which seemed swift and loud. And today she smelled quite pleasantly of rose water.

The pale blob of Mlle. Rosen's face was right at the edge of Candida's vision, but quite clear; there was no excuse— no excuse at all—for pretending not to notice as she slowly leaned forward and brought her face closer. Candida saw it coming, and felt her heart begin to quicken its beat. She went on reading, stumbling over ordinary, simple words. Mlle. Rosen made no attempt to correct her now.

It was a tender, momentary gesture: merely the laying of a cheek against Candida's shoulder, where her dark hair tumbled over the coarse-textured uniform blazer; but it was a gesture that could only be rejected overtly; merely to pretend it had not happened—as Candida did—was only to be taken as a shy and oblique acceptance.

But that wasn't all of it.

Over ten years later, she said to herself, I'm able to admit to myself that I deliberately led her on. I sat in a particular sort of way, with my profile turned just so, and did pretty things like entwining my fingers in my hair while I was reading. To entice her.

And when I went home that evening—and I knew she wanted to kiss me good night—I danced along the street, full of the secret knowledge that there was someone, however unattractive, who loved me and wanted me in a way that was different from anything I'd known from Mummy.

I destroyed her . . .

"There she is—the slut!"

The women came out of an archway in front of her. Big women, middle-aged women, in raincoats and pixie hoods, carrying large handbags.

"She's been parading around here for the last half-hour!"

"Sizing up her prospects on *our* beat!"

"Get her!"

They came at Candida together, handbags swinging. One heavy bag took her on the side of the mouth. She reeled back against the archway, and felt the salty taste of blood. One of the women seized a handful of her hair, jerking her head forward to meet a handful of raking fingernails. Candida twisted herself free as they clawed at her neck.

Then she was running.

◀ TEN ▶

SHE HAD WALKED for miles, uncaring, along the *grands boulevards*, and she was in the little street fair near the Porte Saint Denis; among the blaring music and the smell of simmering vanilla advertising the candy stalls; a dark girl with a withdrawn expression, and a coat collar drawn up to hide a lacerated neck. Frightened now of the quiet streets, she had found a new anonymity among the faceless crowds.

She came abreast of a shooting gallery: spinning lights, colored balls rising on jets of water, crack of shots and the tang of burned powder. A lone sailor with a red pom-pom on his cap was arguing with the proprietor for the possession of a kewpie doll; the latter shrugged his shoulders and capitulated. The sailor took his shooting prize and grinned amiably about him. He saw Candida passing, and tottered forward with a drunken whoop.

"For you—I won it for you, see?" He thrust the kewpie doll into her hands.

"Thank you," she said.

He saluted her gravely, turned about and weaved away through the crowds.

She went on her way, holding the doll tightly to her, like some kind of talisman.

Still holding it, she passed—unknowingly—under the noses of a parked carload of Haquin's plainclothesmen at the edge of the fair. And she passed unrecognized. They had an excellent description of her—but who expects to find a runaway murder suspect wandering the streets with a ridiculous kewpie doll in her arms?

The time by the ormulu clock under the Napoleonic print was two-thirty.

"Miss Hammersley isn't fit to be interviewed?" growled Haquin.

"No, Chief," said Martin, who had just been to inquire. "For one thing, she had a lot to drink before she came in, and then the news about Stanton sent her off into hysterics. The doc's given her something to put her right out till morning."

"I want to see her before the Scotland Yard fellows do," said Haquin. "We really must have our own records straight, even if—as seems likely—the outcome of this case is settled under British jurisdiction. See if you can get her down here as soon as she wakes up in the morning, will you?"

Martin nodded, sat down opposite his superior and opened the cardboard portfolio.

"Read me that last bit again" said Haquin. "That last statement of Lubbock's, please."

"'I knew Jerry Stanton well,'" read Martin. "'At one time, better than almost anyone. He liked women. They flattered his ego. He preferred them pretty, sexy, and attractive—but he'd settle for them just plain sexy, if pushed. That was only half of him, Superintendent. He was ambisexual—what you might call AC/DC. And when it came right down to it, the homosexual half of him was the most meaningful, and the nearest to his true personality.

"'I'm sure—and he confided as much many times when we shared the flat—that he could never have faced marriage, and for this reason: it would have disgusted him to have had to share a bathroom with a girl.'"

"Mmmm."

"I wonder if Miss Jeans knew about that?" said Martin.

Haquin shrugged. "Perhaps not. I must say, she strikes me as a very ingenuous person, who has led a very sheltered and restricted upbringing. Ambisexuality would be an extremely sophisticated concept for such a person to handle. I take it there's no further news from the streets?"

"Nothing, Chief. The usual false alarms, and quite a few women picked up for loitering. No Miss Jeans. Not yet."

Haquin rammed his hands deeply into his trousers' pockets and sat back.

"She interests me, that girl. You know that, don't you, Martin? I would give a lot to be able to do more than merely turn her and her companions safely over to the Scotland Yard fellows."

"Solve the murder, do you mean, Chief? But all the material evidence—such as there is—is over in England, where the crime was committed. And surely there isn't much doubt that the girl Jeans is the murderess."

"Forget that. Listen . . ."—Haquin took out a pencil and reached for a notepad—". . . let's take a long straight look at what we have so far. Go through the dossier and give me a summary of the salient facts. Start with the the discovery of the hand at Orly."

Martin began, and Haquin's pencil began the first convolutions of an elaborate doodle on the blank page before him.

". . . the preliminary pathological report told us that the amputation was the work of a layman, and that the hand had been amputated either from a living body or at the time of death, and that it had been subjected to light refrigeration. We passed this on to Scotland Yard, together with the statements from Lubbock, Hammersley, and Jeans."

"Scotland Yard soon had the answer," said Haquin.

"They telexed back within—let's see—two hours," said Martin. "Following up Candida Jeans's association with Stanton, they found that he'd not been into work that day. Breaking into his flat, they found his body. Cause of death was a stab wound immediately below the sternum, and the murder weapon—a bodkin or hatpin—was still in place. The body was minus head and both hands. Estimated time of death, around midnight on Saturday. There were traces that the hands and head had been put into the refrigerator. . . ."

"In order," said Haquin, "to be in a fresh condition to be brought to Paris on the Monday, for—you will remember—it was an oppressively hot weekend throughout northern Europe."

Now she was wandering the boulevards, keeping with the last of the late-night crowds; a fragment of human flotsam, moving with the receding tide. Now all the restaurants were closed, and most of the music halls and cabarets. From time to time, she met up with a stream of revelers turning out of some night spot—laughing and singing perhaps—and moved with them till they dispersed and went their different ways, leaving her alone again and vulnerable.

The night wind brought a flurry of chill rain. She shivered, and pulled her coat collar closer.

Alone. Adrift in the heart of a great city, she had never before been so aware of solitude. And, as her mood shifted, and she became estranged from her own shut-in world of recollections, her mind searched around for the image of a face, or a voice: someone to share with. . . .

Mummy? No. Call for her in vain. They took her away from me in that hideous crematorium chapel on the hill. There's no return for the already-dead.

But, before I destroyed you, Mummy—like I destroyed all the others—was there a time when we might have shared?

If I'd gone to you that night and explained about Mlle. Rosen: admitted that you were right about me, and begged for your help and understanding, would it have changed anything?

It was past four o'clock.

"Whichever way you look at it," said Martin, "we don't have a lot to go on, Chief. And it will be the Scotland Yard fellows who find the answers when they get these people back to England."

The old night porter elbowed open the door, laid down another coffee and lager, saluted Haquin and went out again.

Martin continued: "There are the hands—and now the head, of course—but they add up to nothing, save confirmation of identity. We've still no idea why, or how, this grotesque charade was carried out—only that it was carried out by one or all of these three people, and almost certainly by Jeans."

Haquin had, by now, covered the page of the notepad with elaborate swirls and cartouches. In one of the cartouches, he had written a few lines of blank verse; and now he read them aloud:

"Thou didst treat me as a harlot . . .
I still live, but thou art dead,
and thy head belongs to me . . ."

"Pardon me, Chief?" said Martin, surprised.

"Salome," said Haquin. "That's a quotation from Oscar Wilde's *Salome*, as best as I can recall it. He originally wrote it in French, you know, for Sarah Bernhardt."

Martin combated his sudden puzzlement and unease by addressing himself to his coffee. Haquin continued—more than half to himself:

"As to the question of why, there are interesting precedents. Salome, for one. Rejected by Jokanaan in life, she demanded his head, and—in Wilde's version—made mock of it in the form of a love fetish."

"Are you suggesting it was like that with the Jeans girl, Chief?" asked Martin.

"Salome and Jokanaan," said Haquin. "Then there was Judith and Holofernes, which is the story of a woman who ensnared a man with her beauty, and then killed him. She took away his head. In her case, it was to prove to everyone that he was dead."

"That motive would hardly apply in this case," said Martin wryly.

"There was Joanna the Mad," said Haquin. "Heiress of the Spanish Empire, who loved her husband with a jealous and consuming passion, and almost certainly murdered him. She spent the rest of her life wandering from one to another of her gloomy castles in Spain—with the embalmed body of her husband to keep her company."

"I don't think I'm following your line of reasoning, Chief," confessed Martin.

"As to why a woman would carry round with her the remains of her murdered lover, there are almost as many reasons as there are cases," said Haquin. "But I suppose they all add up to the same motivation: necrolatry—the worship of the dead. So much for why. I don't think our answer lies there, Martin."

"I suppose not," said Martin sulkily.

"Try—how?"

"That's a real puzzler, Chief. The first hand was easy, of course. She carried that with her cabin luggage, and it was found by the Orly Customs officer. But supposing it hadn't been found? What then?"

"Forget that for the moment. Consider the second hand."

"That's what I simply can't understand. By Monday evening, we knew all about Stanton's murder and the removal of the hands and head. While the three of them were out at dinner, we searched all three of their rooms with a fine-toothed comb, and found nothing. Yet on Tuesday night, the Jeans girl went out on her own and buried the second hand in a flower bed on the Champs Élysées. Where had it been in the meantime?"

Haquin formed his unaccommodating features into a beam of approval at his assistant.

"That's very good, Martin," he said. "You're asking the right questions now. And what about the head?"

"Yes! Where has that been till tonight? We knew of its possibly being in Paris—and, indeed, Scotland Yard particularly asked us to do nothing but keep the three of them under continuous surveillance till it showed up—but where has *that* been hidden since Monday?"

Haquin drained his lager glass. Walking over to the window, he drew aside the curtain and looked out into the darkness. Dawn was not far away.

"Did she do it, Chief?" asked Martin.

"Possibly," said Haquin. "You know, she fascinates me,

Martin. There's something about her. Perhaps all the great classical murderesses had it. I wouldn't know; the way my career has worked out, I've met so few murderesses."

"She must be insane, in any event," said Martin, "to have carted the bits and pieces around."

Haquin ignored that; continued looking out of the window.

"Perhaps she murdered Stanton," he said. "But that's not to say she *knows* she's done it."

The turn of the tide in the great city, and the watershed between day and night, was almost imperceptible. Despite all her fears, there was no moment of complete solitude. While the shutters and bars were going up outside some late-night cabaret, the lights were going on in a café down the street. The lingering smell of vanilla gave way to that of freshly roasted coffee. The last of the revelers rubbed shoulders with blue-denimed workmen. The overhead lighting dimmed, and the water tankers washed the streets in preparation for the new day.

She found a quiet café on a turning off the Boulevard Haussmann, where workaday Parisians stood at the zinc counter with their newspapers, downing coffee and cracking hard-boiled eggs. No one took the slightest notice of the girl with the kewpie doll who took her coffee to a corner table on her own.

She had only to turn her head to face her own close-up reflection on the wall of engraved mirror glass. Her eyes were dark-rimmed and dead, and her skin pallid with fatigue. The shower of rain had dried on her hair, leaving it in rat tails.

Sonia Hammersley woke up at first light of dawn and rang down to the reception desk, demanding coffee and aspirin.

Haquin was informed of this, and he sent Inspector Martin up to Room 44 with an urgent request for Miss Hammersley to come down, if she was fit enough.

"Tell her I need some information from her which may lead to the arrest of Miss Jeans," said Haquin dryly. "If that doesn't bring her, nothing will."

She came into the manager's office a quarter of an hour later, wearing sweater and slacks, with her hair wrapped in a scarf of raw Indian silk. Her eyes were hidden behind dark glasses. She seemed unsteady on her feet; only Martin's guiding hand prevented her from bumping into the back of the easy chair that had been set out for her.

"You wanted to ask me something?" Her voice was hoarse and strained.

"Yes, Miss Hammersley." Haquin made considerable play of running his pencil along several paragraphs of the type-written sheet before him. "Let me see—ah, yes . . ." He looked up. "When you arrived here at the hotel on Monday afternoon, after leaving your two companions behind at the Quai des Orfèvres, you made a telephone call to the London publishing house for which you work—Grave Vale Press, is it not?"

"Yes."

"Why did you do that, Miss Hammersley?"

"Why?" Sonia Hammersley made a brusque gesture with her hands. "Why? It's perfectly obvious. I wanted to put them in the picture about what happened at the airport, before they started getting garbled versions from the news agencies."

"Yes, I'm aware that you had a conversation with a member of the board of directors of Grave Vale Press," said Haquin. "But was that your only—indeed your prime—reason for putting through the call to London?"

Sonia Hammersley groped in her handbag for a packet of

Gauloises, and took one out with unsteady fingers. Inspector Martin's hand materialized round the angle of her cheek, with a cigarette-lighter flame flickering.

"Well, Miss Hammersley?" persisted Haquin.

She blew out a mouthful of smoke.

"I don't follow you."

"I think you do," said Haquin mildly. "However, by way of prompting you, let me put it this way: Was your urgent call to the Grave Vale Press on Monday afternoon in any way connected with the letter which you had been handed on your arrival at the hotel—the letter addressed to Miss Jeans, which was given into your care?"

The disks of smoked black glass told him nothing, but her voice indicated that his shot had found its mark.

"Did—*she*—tell you about that?"

"Miss Jeans? No! I should tell you, Miss Hammersley," said Haquin, "that our inquiries relating to this case have been much, much more extensive than they may have appeared to you. For instance, while you were dining on Monday evening, the letter in question was found—opened—in your room. And photographed."

He held up a sheet of paper.

"Well?" Her chin came up, and there was an edge of defiance in her voice. "So what?"

"Did you ring Grave Vale Press on Monday afternoon, at about four o'clock, primarily in order to speak to Jeremy Stanton, the art director of *Focal* magazine?"

"Yes!"

"With what result?"

"They—his secretary and his assistant art man—told me he hadn't come into the office that day."

"And what was your reaction to that?"

"I thought they were lying!" grated Sonia Hammersley. "And I bloody well told them so!"

"And why should they be lying?"

"Monday," said Sonia Hammersley wearily, "was press day on the magazine. This is the day when the art director —any art director—just *might* stay away for serious illness, but it would have to be well into the burst appendix or cerebral hemorrhage class. Jeremy Stanton is—was—the sort of art director who would have dragged himself in on press day if he'd been dying."

"So what, then, did you think?" asked Haquin.

No reply.

He held up the photocopy of the letter: "Following on what you'd read in this letter, you thought it likely that Jeremy Stanton was in the office all the time, but was deliberately avoiding having to speak with you."

"Yes!"

Haquin relaxed in his seat and folded his arms.

"But, as we know, you were quite wrong, were you not?" he said. "Jeremy Stanton was not in his office on Monday for the very good reason that he was lying dead in his flat."

"OH!" Sonia Hammersley buried her face in her hands; thrusting her fingers behind the dark lenses and kneading her eyes till the glasses fell off into her lap. Her eyes were red and swollen from many hours of crying. She blinked and bowed her head with embarrassment as she rummaged in her handbag for a handkerchief.

"I'm making a fool of myself," she said huskily.

"Not in the slightest," said Haquin.

"Is that all—can I go now?"

"There's just one more point," said Haquin. "It concerns a phrase in the letter that mystifies me slightly. It's open to several interpretations. It seems to me that you—who must have read the letter very carefully many times—must be able to help."

"What phrase is this?"

Haquin picked up the photocopy again.

"This is the part," he said. "Referring to his having made a decision to break off his association with Miss Jeans, Stanton goes on to say: 'No need to trample around in the mire and drag out the reasons why. There's only one reason, anyhow. And it's nothing either of us can do anything about—and least of all you, as I'm perceptive enough to appreciate.' Now, what did he mean by that? What was this reason for his nearly breaking off the relationship?"

Sonia Hammersley had put on the dark glasses again. Her gaze was as blank and cold as her voice.

"Because he couldn't get her into bed! Because, as a woman, she's a complete phony. A washout. A dried-up, frigid little bitch hiding behind a pretty face!"

"You know this for sure?" asked Haquin.

"I had it from Jeremy Stanton himself," said Sonia Hammersley. "We used to laugh our heads off about a story of him inveigling her into a hotel bedroom in Brighton. In the defense of her precious honor, the bitch went for him with a knife or a pair of scissors—I forget which. He mentioned the scar on his arm later on in that same letter."

"Nevertheless, Stanton was greatly attracted to her," said Haquin. "The letter proves it."

Sonia Hammersley shrugged. "He spent all of that Saturday evening with me at my flat," she said. "Then went straight home and wrote that load of mawkish rubbish to her. There was a strong streak of the pervert in Jeremy Stanton."

"That I have already heard," murmured Haquin.

The faces shifted across her mind: faces of those she had trapped and destroyed.

Mummy had been right: the evil had been born in her,

and it was no use fighting the inherited taint any longer. Down through the years—beginning with the temptation of poor Mlle. Rosen—the evil had grown stronger inside her, leading her to destroy others; now it was destroying her, too. Her mind was going.

Am I mad?

She silently addressed her reflection in the mirrored wall.

Did I go mad that night when I knew that Jeremy had lied to me and gone with another woman? The murderous impulse that made me drive the paper-knife into the table, was that the beginning? Did my madness lead me to find and destroy him, for wanting to abandon me?

"How did I kill you, Jeremy? Did I hurt you terribly much?" she said aloud.

"Pardon, mam'selle?" A waiter, collecting the cups and glasses at the next table, spun round in surprise. "Is there something I can get you?"

She smiled. "No, thank you."

It was dawn, but a new night was already closing in about her. She met the reflection of her smile when she stood up. It was unlike any expression she had ever seen on her face before: a closed-mouth smile of serenity that looked out beyond pain, beyond death, beyond all doubts.

Smiling still, and curiously light-headed, she walked out of the café and into the dawn, with the kewpie doll in her arms.

◄ ELEVEN ►

AT THE FAR END of the Pont d'Iena was a roast-chestnut stand shaped like a locomotive; its polished brasswork reflected a semicircle of grave-eyed children.

The morning rush-hour traffic streamed along the Quai Branly, and she had to wait, with a small crowd of pedestrians, behind the outstretched arm of a policeman. When he lowered his arm and let them cross, he met her eye and smiled, for she was young and pretty and had a serene smile that seemed to embrace everyone and everything.

She crossed the *pavé* and walked slowly into the wide sweep of open space beyond. Above her were the massive iron arches of the great Tower; above them, the tapering shaft that soared to its gray climax in the sky. A party of seminarists, pale faces above black alpaca, trotted behind a tight-lipped priest. The boys at the tail end gaped at her, huge-eyed; and one of them muttered something to his fellow that set them both sniggering.

There was a balloon seller: an old woman with a mass of multicolored balloons that swayed in the wind like the painted sails of a tall ship. She watched, suddenly entranced, as children swarmed around the woman. When they raced away, each with a bobbing colored balloon, she joined the queue at the ticket desk.

She had exactly enough money left in her pocket to pay.

The lift to the first platform rolled stiffly up a sharp incline inside the trunk of one of the great supporting arches, and it was tightly packed and smelling of garlic and Gauloises. Directly in front of her were a boy and a girl; his arm round her, eyes to eyes, silently communicating.

"Why do you carry a doll, mam'selle?"

It was a little girl of about seven. She wore a pink velvet dress and brown button boots. Her parents stood near. Country people. The jaws of their red, bovine faces munched at long sandwiches.

She smiled. "Because it was given to me."

"Who gave it to you—your boyfriend?"

All eyes turned to regard her. Bovine jaws froze in mid-motion.

"Yes, he's a sailor—with a red pom-pom on his cap."

The lift glided to a smooth halt, and the doors swung open. She walked out onto the crowded deck of the first platform. There was another lift, which meant another wait, another imprisonment in a sea of regarding faces. Better to walk.

At the first few turns of the iron stairs, she was aware of the constant motion of the Tower. It was hardly perceptible: a vague, half-imagined vertigo, like the sensation after a long sea voyage, when the earth seems to heel gently like the deck of a ship. She moved quite quickly up the stairs, steadying herself against the hand rails. Round and round. Up and up. With every turn, Paris dropped further away below her;

became grayer and more remote. And the higher she went, the more blustery grew the wind.

There were quite a few people on the second, smaller platform. Despite the warmth of spring sun, the wind was chilly up there. Men pulled up their coat collars, and women found sheltered corners to put on their head scarves. The wind and the steel rigging gave the scene a nautical quality. People walked briskly up and down, to keep warm, their clothes and hair fluttering—like in a holiday seascape by Boudin. Some crowded the outer rails of the platform and pointed out the landmarks to each other: Notre Dame, riding the center of the river like the dramatic hulk of an old ship; the knoll of Montmartre, crowned by the iced wedding cake of Sacré Coeur; the Bois de Boulogne a smudge of blue-green through the haze of the great city.

No one took the slightest notice of the dark-haired girl with the kewpie doll.

There was a police radio van parked in the narrow street outside the hotel: a large affair that called for warning signs, orange markers, and a couple of officers to direct the traffic. It caused a considerable rush-hour bottleneck in the Madeleine area.

The missing girl having evaded—in the face of all probability—the massive street search that had been carried on during the night, Superintendent Haquin was caught between the Scylla of staying in his makeshift operational headquarters at the hotel, and the Charybdis of being caught halfway back to the Quai des Orfèvres in the rush hour with the possibility of news coming through that Candida Jeans had been located.

The near certainty that the fugitive would speedily be found in the daylight hours—added to the unattractive prospect of awaiting the result of a city-wide search from his temporary cubbyhole in police headquarters—decided Haquin to stay right where he was, till midmorning, at any rate. The simple statistics of the job would dictate, by midday, that the major effort be switched to searching for the girl's corpse.

Meanwhile, there was breakfast coffee and *croissants* in the manager's office, with the radio van—a direct link with the searchers—in sight outside the window, and Martin dodging in every few minutes with gobbits of news and information.

He came in again.

"One more thing," said Haquin. "Will you make sure that Lubbock is standing by this morning? If and when she turns up, I want him around. And if it's necessary to go to her, I want him with me."

"Right, Chief. He's sitting in the lobby, anyhow, looking like one big screaming nerve end."

"What about the Hammersley girl?"

Martin rolled his eyes. "My God! I came in to tell you about that. It seems she'd been having cognac with her coffee, and it's warmed up her last night's booze. They've just taken her upstairs, but not before she had an hysterical outburst in the breakfast room: told everyone who cared to listen—and that was everyone—that Miss Jeans was a murderess and a vampire and the lord knows what else."

Before Haquin could comment, there was a tap on the window. It was one of the officers on duty outside. He looked excited, and was pointing urgently to the radio van.

Alone of all the people on the second platform of the Tower, she avoided the outer rail, where the outward sweep of the supporting piers and their iron latticework marked the view of the ground immediately below. Instead, she walked over to the inner rail. There, in the center of the four soaring shafts of the Tower, was a vast open space.

She looked over and down. Below her was an unimpeded drop to the ground.

Like a segmented worm, a broken line of sightseers dribbled across the space below. When they got to the middle, all their faces turned upward: a sudden sprinkling of pink dots. They moved on; and then the balloon seller passed below, followed by some children and a dog.

She watched it all quite detachedly, with no terror or vertigo—and with no sense of involvement. The ground below seemed very close to her. Just one step to oblivion.

After a while, she turned her back on the void, leaned against the rail and looked across the wide deck of the platform, where the people walked to and fro, or stood and stared out over the city.

Detached, serene, and quite unhurried, she began to cast the promenading strangers in the roles of people who had acted out their given parts in her life's brief dream. . . .

"The girl with the glasses is Sonia," she whispered, "who'll never forgive me for that letter Jeremy wrote. Don't hate me too much, Sonia. You didn't really need him. The loss is all mine. . . ."

If anyone had paid more than a moment's passing attention to her—and no one did—they might have thought: what an attractive and interesting-looking girl, standing there with her kewpie doll, and that rather old-fashioned smile on her lips.

"The man with the craggy face is really Superintendent Haquin without his limp, and the children with him are Susan and Jennifer, who don't play in our garden on Saturday afternoons any more, because Mummy's worried that

I'll pick up their common accents. And, more than anything, I must please Mummy.

"They'll all come past me, sooner or later. One by one. Poor Mlle. Rosen, poor Jeremy—and all the rest.

"I'll wait for Mummy to come. She's the most important. And after I've told her how sorry I am for everything I've done . . ."

Inspector Martin took the Boulevard Malesherbes and the Boulevard Haussmann on screaming tires, with the siren going all the way, and two motorcycle outriders. They arrived outside the café just off the boulevard, and he and Haquin went to quiz the crew of a patrol car who had radioed in the report. There were three of them, all plainclothesmen from the judicial police, and they were taking a statement from a waiter.

"What is it, then, Contindin?" asked Haquin.

"It's her, all right, Chief," said one of them. "Came in here just after they opened this morning and stayed— how long?"

"Till past eight," supplied the waiter. "Drank nothing but a cup of coffee in all that time, and then she . . ."

"She left without paying," said the officer Contindin. "This fellow didn't see her slip out, but noticed she'd gone immediately afterward."

"I ran to the corner of the boulevard," said the waiter, "but she'd disappeared."

"There it might have ended, Chief," said Contindin, "but we decided to do a spot check of the cafés along the boulevards, and this fellow recognized the copy of her passport photo at once."

Haquin eyed the waiter speculatively: he did not look the perceptive type, but it was worth trying.

"How did she strike you, this girl?" he asked the waiter. "What sort of person did you take her for?"

The reaction came without hesitation. The man tapped his head with his forefinger.

"Dotty!" he said firmly. "I've come across her sort before, and they've all ended up by being taken off in a van. Spent a lot of time looking at herself in the mirror. Had a silly, vacant smile on her face, and talked to herself—in English," he added as if by way of a clincher.

Another patrol car crossed the boulevard and slid to a halt nearby, its two-note siren still bleating.

"They've been checking her trail," explained Contindin.

A young plainclothesman got out, and looked impressed to see Haquin.

"We've found out which way she went, sir," he said. And he pointed back across the boulevard, to the street opposite. "That way. A gang of road menders spotted her passing just after she left the café. Walking quite slowly and carrying a kewpie doll."

"Yes, I forgot to tell you that," said the waiter. "She had this kid's doll with her. That was another thing that made her look five centimes short of a franc."

"Something the matter, Chief?" asked Martin.

Haquin was looking across the boulevard, the way Candida Jeans had gone. The road opposite ran straight, and the buildings at each side made a framework for a rectangle of cloud-banked sky. Rising above the distant rooftops at the far end of the street was the slim gray pencil of the great Tower.

Haquin wrenched open the car door and clambered in, dragging his aluminum leg after him. Hilary Lubbock was sitting in the back.

Martin gunned the Citroën into reverse. He did not need to ask for any directions; the same idea had occurred to him.

Descending lift loads had thinned out the people on the second platform. Now there were only six or seven, and her game of charades was dying for lack of characters.

"I'll wait," she whispered, "for one more lift load to come up, and if Mummy isn't on it, I shall go without seeing her."

They had paraded before her in this end-game of her life: most of the main characters and the supernumeraries, and she had had a few words of regret for them all. But no one had appeared who looked the way Mummy had used to look, in all her pale-skinned, blue-eyed beauty and her petite slimness. There aren't many like her, she thought ruefully. Neither now nor at any time in the past. No one could ever replace irreplaceable Mummy.

But—just in case—one more lift . . .

She stood leaning against the inner rail, with the kewpie doll tucked under one arm. And the lift crawled up toward the second platform, inside one of the great, fretted uprights. But when it reached there, and the doors came open, there was no one inside but a party of nuns.

The charade was over.

She turned and looked down into the void beneath the Tower, and saw—*her.*

Walking quite quickly across the open space far below; and even from that distance and at that angle, she could see the marcelled hair and the pale blue pillbox hat that was just like one of Mummy's; and the shadow showed her to be slim and small.

"*Mummy! . . . Mummy!*"

Candida Jeans cried out in a loud voice, and changed her grip on the rail. In doing so, she fumbled the kewpie doll.

It seesawed for an instant on the top of the rail—and then fell over.

It fell slowly, cartwheeling over and over in a completely lifelike manner, arms and legs stiffly extended. And it fell straight, till it reached the level of the four great supporting arches; there the wind reshaped its course and drove it against the massive ironwork. From where she stood, she clearly saw the kewpie doll decapitated by the impact. Body and head rebounded from the ironwork and fell together the last few meters. The pink pieces were quite visible from the second platform: they landed some distance from the woman in the pale blue pillbox hat, who did not even turn round.

Candida Jeans buried her face in her hands and shuddered with the horror of what she had seen. She was still standing by the rail when Inspector Martin and Hilary Lubbock reached the second platform, having run up the stairs.

Lubbock put his arm round her, and she looked up into his face. It was then she remembered that it had never occurred to her to find his substitute character for her strange game of charades, and for this reason: that nothing had ever passed between them for which she had any cause for regret.

◄ TWELVE ►

THE CLOUDS had cleared away by eleven o'clock, and Paris lay under sunshine. The heat brought out the color, the summery dresses, and the shirt sleeves; it filled the outside tables in the Champs Élysées; it caused the mingled odors of car exhaust and burned tire rubber to hang over the streets.

At about this time, the workmen redecorating the Quai des Orfèvres decided to call a one day's strike to draw attention to their grievances. Their departure coincided with the arrival of the three detectives who had been sent from Scotland Yard to wind up any further inquiries they might find necessary in Paris and to accompany—no euphemism was intended, no warrant of arrest had been issued—Candida Jeans and her companions back to London.

Martin had met the Britishers—a superintendent and two inspectors—at Orly, and had given them an up-to-the-minute account of the morning's events during the drive to headquarters. Arriving there, he took them to a spare conference room, where he was able to show them a map of Paris on which Candida Jeans's comings and goings had been traced from the moment of her arrival in Paris, with a different color for each day. The meandering red line for today, Thursday, ended with a cross beside the Eiffel Tower. The Scotland Yard men were impressed.

They were impressed, also, by the facilities which were granted them in the matter of interviewing Hilary Lubbock and Sonia Hammersley, both of whom were immediately produced, together with English-speaking stenographers and soundproof interview rooms. Sonia Hammersley volunteered a thousand-word statement, in which she specifically accused Candida Jeans of murdering Jeremy Stanton, for the motive of insane jealousy, having attempted it once before in a Brighton hotel room on a date unknown to her. Lubbock firmly but politely refused to make any comment.

Next, the British superintendent said he would like to see the woman Jeans, and also the officer who had been in charge of the case.

It was then that Martin took refuge behind a front of excessive Gallicism: with a lot of shoulder hunching and with discernibly worsened accent and slipshod syntax, he informed the other that the woman Jeans was under sedation following the traumatic shock of a possible suicide attempt from the Eiffel Tower, and that Superintendent Haquin had regrettably been called away. Both, he said, would be available within a few hours. After lunch, perhaps.

In fact, Haquin was sitting in his cluttered cubbyhole of an office, with the case file before him. The margins of all the sheets of paper in the file were covered in his spidery handwriting. It seemed to him that he had extracted the last scintilla of information and inspiration from the bland account of the comings and goings of Candida Jeans, her companions, and the murdered man.

He looked at his watch, then at the internal phone that stood at his elbow.

Only one chance now, he thought. And not much time for it, at that. By all the rules of the game, it wasn't even his case any more. If that phone didn't ring before Martin brought the Britishers back from an expensive lunch on the Directorate of Judicial Police, someone else would have to find the key to Candida Jeans.

She was with the doctor with the long face and the compassionate eyes; the same one who had cared for her the first time on—was it Monday?—it seemed a lifetime ago. They had brought her to his private office, which was a little room along the corridor from the clinic where she had lain the first time.

She was sitting in a large leather-covered armchair in front of his desk. The curtains were drawn, and the only light was a desk lamp that threw an island of brightness between them. The rumble of distant traffic came from beyond the window. She felt strangely peaceful and relaxed.

He shifted in his chair and smiled across at her; he looked like a benign billy goat.

"Feeling better?" he asked. "Are the tablets taking effect?"

She nodded. "Yes. They must have been very strong."

"Not really. Just powerful enough to provide a buttress against what your national poet described as the slings and arrows of outrageous fortune. The effect will wear off all too soon, I'm afraid. But I'll give you another dose to take with you when you go."

She turned the question over in her mind before she uttered it: strangely, it held no terror.

"Are they sending me back to England?"

"You're going back with the others this afternoon, as originally arranged. You have seats booked on a plane, haven't you?"

"Shall I be under arrest?"

"I don't think so."

The traffic noises had almost died away. In the silence that followed, she thought she could hear the ticking of both their watches.

She cast around for something to say. It seemed absurd, to be sitting face to face with this perfectly nice man, who obviously liked her and was anxious to help in any way he could, with neither of them saying a word.

"I—I didn't go up the Eiffel Tower to do away with myself," she said.

He nodded.

"It was like the end of a journey," she said. "I walked around all night, you know, thinking about things. And I knew that, in the morning, I was going to make some kind of an end. It was daylight, and I came out of this café, to see the Tower in the distance. It seemed to beckon me."

"Please go on," he said.

She leaned her head back against the cool leather and closed her eyes. What she was saying to him seemed to be hastening the relaxation of tension that was taking place in her mind.

"When I got up there," she said, "I had no sense of fear, yet all the time it seemed to me that something—and it may have been my life—was going to end shortly. Yet there was no hurry. I had plenty of time. Time to play a game."

"A game? Tell me about this game," he said.

She explained about the strange charade, where people

from her life had been personified by passersby. He smiled when she mentioned Superintendent Haquin.

"Why my good friend Haquin?" he asked.

"Because—because I nearly turned to him for help the other day, and I regret that I didn't, because I've the impression that he really wanted to help me."

"And who else came into your charade?"

"Two little girls I was once friendly with, but whom I treated rather shabbily. And someone else. . . ."

"Yes?"

"She—was a French teacher I had at school. There was an embarrassing situation connected with her and Mummy and me. I really don't want to talk about it."

He made no comment, but looked down at his hands.

"She—was in love with me," said Candida Jeans. "Mummy, who was very straitlaced and unworldly, found out about it. Secretly, she blamed me for leading Mlle. Rosen on . . ."—she took a deep breath—". . . and, in fact, she wasn't far wrong. I did lead her on, in a way. I enjoyed her admiration."

"And you feel guilty for having done that?"

"Yes, I do."

"Tell me about some other people in your charade."

"Sonia Hammersley."

"Yes?"

"I think she may have loved Jeremy Stanton, after her fashion," she said. "He was the sort of person with whom it was ridiculously easy to fall in love, or think you'd fallen in love. There was so much of oneself in him. By that, I mean there was a lot of the feminine in his make-up. He had a woman's perceptiveness, so that he would always know if you were tired or feeling on edge. On the other hand, he could be brutally masculine and totally inconsiderate. Yes, I think Sonia may have been in love with him."

"And you have guilt feelings about that?"

"I know now that he would never have left me for her," she said.

"Did you love him?"

"I needed him. I think there was a part of his make-up that needed me, or someone like me. With a relationship like that, the question of love hardly entered into it." She saw her fingers tense against the arms of the chair, and felt a prickle of unease disturb her drug-induced placidity. "And now, are you going to ask me if I killed him?"

"No," he said. "I'd rather you told me about the rest of the people in your charade."

"There weren't many more," she said. "And by the time I found someone to impersonate Mummy, the game was really over. Mummy was the most important, but she never really came into the game."

"Who else, then?"

After a while, she said: "There was Uncle Bernard."

"Who was he?"

"An old friend of Mummy's," she said. "In a way, I suppose he was a kind of admirer of hers. I'd known him all my life. He was always very kind to me, a sort of substitute father-figure. And then . . ."

"Yes. Go on."

"And then, when I was thirteen, he got me alone in the house one night, and tried to assault me."

The sound of the traffic took over again, and now it was too loud for her to hear the tick of their watches.

"I'm rather puzzled," he said presently. "It seems to me that the people you assembled for your charade were all people about whom you have guilt feelings. Feelings of regret and feelings of sorrow. How does Uncle Bernard fit into this pattern? In spite of what he attempted on you, you feel some compassion, because of the kindness he once showed you, perhaps?"

Her hands were trembling now. She had the greatest difficulty in telling him about that night at St. Aubyn and its appalling aftermath.

The road wound out of the city to the crematorium on the hill; and she had made the long, slow drive in one of the undertaker's limousines, with no recollection of the journey or of the three silent strangers who had traveled with her.

Now they all stood with their mourning black molded by the wind, in an open court flanked by evergreens, before the contemporary-styled chapel with the sham-Gothic chimney rising behind it. One of the faceless strangers said they were early, so they hung back while another party of mourners went on into the chapel behind a coffin that bobbed on the shoulders of four shuffling men. Somebody said: "It doesn't take long."

Candida shivered, and tried to concentrate on the floral tributes that the undertaker's men were laying out on display along one side of the court. She was too far away to read the black-edged cards attached to them. No one was taking any notice of her.

There was a movement at the door of the chapel, and one of the men came out and snapped his fingers. The mourning party broke up into groups of three or four and went slowly forward, pausing at the steps while the coffin covered in purple baize was slide out of the rear of the hearse. The leading cars of yet another funeral were winding up the hill from the gates as Candida followed the rest of them inside.

The chapel smelled of beeswax and arum lilies in the

blue gloom. She took a seat in an empty pew at the back, pressed her fingers against her eyes and pretended to pray.

Piped-organ music faded. She opened her eyes when someone signaled for their attention by clearing his throat.

"At the close of the service, would you please leave the chapel by the door at this end. . . ." The clergyman looked very young and inexperienced, but there was a practiced smoothness about his delivery. He must work at the chapel and do nothing but funerals all day long, she thought.

"Man that is born of woman hath but a short time to live, and is full of misery . . ."

Candida might have run through the rain and darkness, till her terror subsided with weariness, without meeting anyone —in which case the episode would have ended there. Instead, she rushed out of the gate of St. Aubyn and into the arms of a middle-aged couple on their way to a bingo session. Fed on lifetimes of pleasurable Sunday afternoons with juicy newspaper court reports, they reacted with delicious fury to the hysterical, half-stripped schoolgirl.

The man put through an emergency call to the police from the phone box on the corner, then they took the distraught girl back to St. Aubyn, to give the monster a piece of their minds. Uncle Bernard—who opened the front door only after several minutes of their ringing, hammering, and shouting—was cringing on the porch before the invective of his tormentors when the patrol car arrived.

He was never formally charged with the assault. They were all taken to the police station, and a motherly woman police sergeant got some sort of a statement from the weeping girl. While this was happening, Uncle Bernard was in the process of dying.

He asked to go to the lavatory. Within minutes, the

constable waiting outside the door heard his feet drumming
out his agony against the porcelain pedestal. They cut him
down, half-strangled by his own braces, which he had looped
over the flushing lever. They revived him with mouth-to-
mouth contact and artificial respiration; but a hastily summoned police surgeon didn't like the look of the excessive
cyanosis, and sent him to the hospital. Uncle Bernard suffered
a massive embolism in the ambulance on the way there, and
was taken straight to the mortuary.

A man died a natural death from heart failure. The
slender record of his transgression was filed away on a dusty
top shelf.

"Thou knowest, Lord, the secrets of our hearts . . ."

Mummy was in the second pew from the front, her slight
figure pathetically girlish in a black grosgrain coat with a
fur collar; kneeling between her cousin and his wife from
Sheffield. She had not spoken to Candida since that night;
since a patrol car had picked her up from the art-appreciation lecture and brought her to the police station, where
the news had already come through about Uncle Bernard's
death. From there, she had been taken to a nursing home;
and the Sheffield cousin and his wife had arrived the following morning, to cope with St. Aubyn and the ordering of
Candida's life.

Awkwardly, avoiding her glance, the Sheffield cousin had
informed Candida that she must attend the funeral, that it
would be better for all concerned: everything was going
to be buried and forgotten, he said.

So she was here—disregarded among the dead man's relations and friends, the brother Masons, a representative of
the Lord Mayor, someone from the City Chamber of Com-
merce, and someone else from the British Legion; all with

their backs turned toward her and heads bowed in the direction of the intoning clergyman and the purple-covered coffin pointing toward the double doors in the far wall.

"*. . . we therefore commit his body to the ground; earth to earth, ashes to ashes . . .*"

A mechanical whirring, discreetly muted—and the coffin began to roll forward toward the opening doors. Candida closed her eyes and shuddered. She fought to assemble scraps of happy memories related to Uncle Bernard: games in the garden, picnics by the river—but all that came was the image of a saliva-dripping grin.

"*NO-O-O-O!*"

It was a thin, high wail. It brought the clergyman to slack-mouthed silence. There was a scuffle in the second pew, and a clatter of heels on the parquet, as Mummy evaded the Sheffield cousin's grasp, brushed past the clergyman, and seized the end of the moving coffin with her black-gloved hands.

"*It wasn't your fault, Bernard—she drove you to it!*"

There was a general surging toward her. Their horrified whispers of persuasion were drowned by the animal sounds that clamored from her wide-open mouth. An attempt to ease her gently away became more violent and meaningful; one of the men locked his arms round her waist, while another took her arms; her hat fell off and she clawed the empty air when her fingers were dragged away from the purple baize.

One of the undertaker's men gave the coffin a hard shove that sent it skidding over the rollers and into the curtained darkness beyond: he howled to someone out of sight to shut the bloody doors, for Christ's sake.

They were frankly fighting her now. Candida stood all alone at the far end of the chapel, staring across the rows of empty pews, at paunchy middle-aged men slithering over the parquet with a screaming little woman.

At the end of it—and with Candida's permission—the doctor phoned his friend Superintendent Haquin on the internal line. Haquin joined them within a few minutes, took a seat at one end of the desk, and listened to the doctor's résumé of Candida's account.

"She was not your real mother," he said.

"Only my foster-mother," said Candida. "I was told immediately after the funeral—after she had been taken away in the ambulance. . . ."

"Go on, please."

"They told me I was illegitimate. That was why Mummy thought I was tainted with dirt, you see. Because of my real father: a male brute who got some shameless young trollop into trouble—that would have been her reading of the situation, poor Mummy."

"Did you ever see her again?"

"No. Never. I was fostered elsewhere, and they changed my name from Candida Rawlings to Candida Jeans."

"Rawlings—ah—was there ever a Mr. Rawlings?"

"Yes. She never spoke of him, but I think he must have died just before I was born. I can't think that it could have been a very happy marriage."

"She probably found widowhood more to her taste," said Haquin dryly. "Tell me more about the Jeans family."

"They were very warm, outgoing people," said Candida. "They helped me to face up to the outside world. After all that had happened, it had become a place of terror for me. They had a girl of their own, and the two of us were sent to dancing classes. It was through dancing that I was introduced to modeling."

The cosseting effect of the drug was wearing off, and all her familiar fears were beginning to return. She looked from one to the other of the two men who were regarding her.

"All that happened ten years ago," she said. "But not a day's gone past in all that time when I haven't remembered what I did to Mummy."

"What did you do?" asked Haquin.

"I drove her insane!" she cried. "Don't you see? She must have loved Uncle Bernard, after her fashion. Because of me, he died a sordid, shameful death."

"Do you really believe that?" asked Haquin. "That it was because of you?"

Candida did not reply. Head bowed, she was picking at the seam of her skirt with her fingernail.

"Or isn't that merely what your foster-mother believed?"

◄ THIRTEEN ►

INSPECTOR MARTIN saw to it that the Scotland Yard men had an excellent lunch, and protracted the meal for as long as he was able, arriving back at the Quai des Orfèvres with his guests just before three o'clock.

Haquin had left word with the duty officers on the door that he was to be called as soon as Martin's car drove into the forecourt; he was in the hall to greet them, and Martin guessed—from his chief's uncharacteristic bonhomie—that all must be well.

And, indeed, so it seemed to be. There had been, said Haquin, an unexpected breakthrough in the case: an entirely new development that called for immediate inquiries to be made to Scotland Yard—and how fortunate that their British colleagues were here to hasten the proceedings from the Paris end. He outlined the details of the new development, as a result of which the British superintendent drafted telex messages for three separate departments of Scotland Yard.

The replies—collated in one message—were back in their hands within the hour:

ONE—MRS EDITH RAWLINGS CERTIFIED INSANE AND COM- MITTED TO HAVERFORD MENTAL HOSPITAL 4.11.60. APPAR- ENT IMPROVEMENT IN CONDITION LED TO DISCHARGE FROM HAVERFORD 17.2.70. TWO—PASSPORT NUMBER 169664 IS- SUED TO MRS RAWLINGS LONDON 10.4.70. THREE—MRS RAWLINGS TRAVELED ON BEA FLIGHT 303 ARRIVING IN PARIS AT 1800 HOURS 20.4.70

"She was only discharged in February, you see," said Haquin, "but she wasted no time over her revenge. It would have taken her no time, of course, to have traced her former foster-daughter; the face of the girl whom she sought to destroy looked out at her from every bookstall. Then it would simply have been a matter of making discreet inquiries at the top model agencies."

"Then she discovered Miss Jeans's association with Stanton," supplied Martin. "And engineered a casual acquaintance with him. He was a great animal lover, wasn't he? She could quickly have got on chatting terms with him by walking a friendly dog past his flat every morning, just as he was leaving."

"Something like that," said Haquin. "In any event, we must presume that she eventually got to know him well enough to learn the details of the Black Look assignment. And in the early hours of last Sunday morning, she called round at his flat, and killed him by driving a hat pin into his chest."

Martin said: "She arrived here on the afternoon plane on Monday, after slipping the first hand into Miss Jeans's box at the airport, while the three of them were at the bar. The rest would have been reasonably easy. Given the life-style of the hotel, it was just a matter of waiting for opportunities: occasions when there was no one at the reception desk, so that she could sneak the key of Miss Jeans's room and plant the second hand in the paper carrier, and afterward the head in the bed."

"Nor was there much risk of her meeting Miss Jeans," said Haquin.

"Exactly, Chief. Apart from the bar and the foyer, there aren't any public rooms. If one made halfway to a deliberate attempt to keep out of someone's way—like avoiding the bar always, and the foyer as much as possible—the chances of meeting them would be very slight indeed."

"Add to that," said Haquin, "ten years in a madhouse must have greatly changed Mrs. Rawlings' appearance—as she is, no doubt, painfully aware."

"I'll go and break the news to that poor girl," said the doctor.

The morning's bright promise had faded, and the great entrance hall was filled with afternoon shadows. Haquin and the doctor were standing together at the top of the staircase when Candida Jeans crossed the floor of the hall below with Hilary Lubbock. Lubbock's arm was round her shoulders. They turned by the swing doors, and saw the two men watching them. Lubbock called out good-bye, and the dark-eyed girl raised her slim hand to wave. The door swung to behind them, and they were gone.

"Will she be all right now?" asked Haquin. "Will she find happiness, I mean?"

"I think so, François," said the other. "The foster-mother's opinion molded her, but she's largely free of that now. The cathartic effect of discovering that the mother-figure tried to destroy her has set her free to a very large extent. At least, that's my opinion."

"She was near to destroying herself this morning," said Haquin.

"I doubt it. She climbed the Tower, and put herself in a suicide situation, as a cry for help. Many of them do it, as you know from your own experience. She went up the Tower and waited there for you to find her. And while she was waiting, she assembled all her guilt feelings, like a row of beads on a string."

"Was there a time, do you think, when she believed that she might have been responsible for the murder of Jeremy Stanton?"

"Perhaps. During the crisis, after her horrific discovery of his head in her bed. She may have believed it as a fact, or symbolically."

"The guilt thing again?"

"Quite. With her kind of guilt complex, she would tend to resolve the inexplicable by taking the guilt upon herself."

"You know, Jean," said Haquin, "she fascinated me right from the first. The only truly beautiful woman I have ever had any dealings with in my life—and, do you know, she was frightened of me, as a man. And this is strange, because I am frightened of women."

"I find that difficult to believe, François," smiled the other.

"It's true. And they always sense it, you know. Even the plainest and least attractive take courage from my weakness and become like arrogant cocottes. But not Candida Jeans. For all her beauty, she was frightened of me as a man. It fascinated me, and I promised myself that I would speak to her about it. But now I never shall."

Martin came running up the stairs toward them, two steps at a time.

"Edith Rawlings is registered at the same hotel as the others, Chief," he said. "You were right. And she's there at this moment."

"Then we'd better go and pick her up," said Haquin.

They found her in the hotel foyer, at a table near the reception desk, chatting amiably with an American lady of about her own age. She was a stout little woman with blue-rinsed hair and dark glasses, dressed—fittingly—in black.

She seemed to be expecting them.